Poor Clare

POOR CLARE

by

L. P. HARTLEY

Quidquid id est, timeo Danaos, et dona ferentes.
Whatever it is, I dread the Greeks, even when
they are bearing gifts.

HAMISH HAMILTON
LONDON

First published in Great Britain, 1968
by Hamish Hamilton Ltd
90 Great Russell Street, London W.C.1
Copyright © 1968 by L. P. Hartley
Second Impression October 1968
Third Impression November 1968
Fourth Impression January 1969
SBN 241 91338 1

Printed in Great Britain
by Ebenezer Baylis and Son Ltd
The Trinity Press, Worcester, and London

Chapter One

'MY POVERTY but not my will consents.' Gilbert appeared to think that his friends would share this scruple of the apothecary in *Romeo and Juliet* and in his letter to me (which must have been more or less a facsimile of his letters to his other friends) he was almost incoherent with apology. Would I like to have the little Girtin? Did I like Girtin's pictures and even if I did, would it go with my other pictures? Perhaps I remembered it—it used to hang in Aunt Clare's sitting-room in Kensington Square, but few of her friends ever penetrated there except by special invitation: no doubt I had, but he couldn't be sure. She kept so many things to herself, including her pictures!

Gilbert was the only child of Clare's only sister. Children she herself had none, brothers she had none; for her nephews and nieces on her husband's side she cared little, though she left them handsome sums of money. But she cherished Gilbert not only because he was her one near relation, but because through thick and thin she believed in his gift as a composer. She wanted him to remember her kindly, she said (it was the only emotional sentence in her will) and she wanted him to remember her by such tokens as would appeal to an artist.

Gilbert did not say whether his aunt, who had been a friend of mine—in so far as she permitted herself friends—had wanted to leave me anything of hers, still less whether she had earmarked the picture for me. In spite of stories that went about, we, her beneficiaries, did not know whether she had meant us to benefit. Still less did we know what Gilbert's rake-off had been. Most people are secretive about money, even practitioners of the arts, and Gilbert, simple and straightforward as he seemed, took after his aunt in this, as she had taken after her husband.

The letter went on to muse about the dead woman—'Poor Clare', as ironically we called her:

'... She was unreasonably proud of my great efforts and my small attainments, which no doubt is partly why she rewarded me so handsomely in her will. You remember her, of course—those luncheons in Kensington Square. She was always a little forbidding and formidable, like other elderly rich women who are surrounded by needy relations and others who are not relations, hoping for a rake-off. She was suspicious of people, indeed she had to be: and going into her house, even on a hot day, was rather like going into a refrigerator, or a Turkish bath in reverse—one went from room to room, getting colder and colder, until at last one was admitted into the Presence. She would rise rather stiffly, reaching for her stick—like many old ladies, she suffered from arthritis, and not only in her bones and muscles but in her spirit. You once said she was shy, and I think she was, but her unresponsiveness went deeper than that: it was an instinct to keep off marauders, even the men who would have liked to marry her, after Alfred's death, and there were several of them, for in her rather frigid way she was very attractive, and she kept her looks—her Empress Theodora looks—long after most women have lost theirs. Emotion is a great destroyer of the features, as you, being a painter, would know better than I—but if she had emotions, she didn't let them reach her face, which became—if you remember—rather mask-like with the years.

'I was never at my ease with her—I doubt if anybody was—but she had a real love of music, and her piano-playing was almost up to professional standards. I used to play duets with her, but though I had perhaps a better sense of the composer's intention, I couldn't enunciate the notes as clearly as she could, and in the difficult parts I sometimes stumbled but she never did. You remember that inscription above a beautiful duet of Schubert's "*Notre amitié est invariable*"? Well, that was true of her and me.

'She never kept men-servants, even in the days when they were

8

comparatively easy to come by: she always had parlour-maids, stiff and starched, with caps and little white aprons, and seeming to belong to a different world from the one she occupied (or didn't occupy). Often I would have liked to say to her "Dear Aunt Clare" (I doubt if she ever knew we spoke of her as "Poor Clare") "Dear Aunt Clare, do let us tell each other something which is of the utmost importance to both of us." And I used to turn over in my mind a pregnant phrase which would have brought us together, but it always eluded me, just as it eludes me in my music, and I could never get it out. Something in the silence and emptiness of those long, high, beautiful rooms, where the honey-coloured ruched silk curtains hung half-way down the windows, daunted me as I suppose it daunted others—yourself included?

'But in spite of that our friendship was "*invariable*" . . .'

*

At that point in his letter Gilbert ceased to recollect the dead woman and spoke instead of what he called 'reciprocity':

'I have never been able to achieve it in my work,' he began; and I knew what he meant. Gilbert, a man of strong feelings, rejoiced in contrasts and conflicts. It was easier for me (as he pointed out) to achieve this reciprocity than it was for him, because my pictures are painted in low tones, which don't need violent contrasts—which wouldn't, indeed, allow them. The colours lean towards each other, the forms repeat each other, with small variations (on which I love to dwell). Whereas his music demanded contrasts as violent as that between the *Allegretto* and the *Presto* of the Moonlight Sonata, and much more cacophonous: his idea of reciprocity was the reciprocity of the boxing-ring: 'You hit me, and I'll hit you'—an exchange of fisticuffs, not the magical, magnetic approach, gradual, yearning, of one sort of feeling wooing another. My notion of art was more modest, certainly less romantic than Gilbert's.

' "Before divine Cecilia came" we are told,' he went on, ' "the world a mass of jarring atoms lay." But the heavenly harmony she is said to have brought down seems to have been short-lived—or at any rate it has vanished from the music that I try to write. I can only think in discords!

'But one's art is of one's life a thing apart, dear Edward, and as I grow older I think wistfully of the harmony, the universal harmony, from which divine Cecilia came and which Dryden and Handel have immortalized. And even if my unhappy temperament makes it impossible for me to realize harmony in music, I may still be able to realize it in life (a reconciliation, peace with God, to put it ambitiously) founded on reciprocity. I owe my friends far more, in every way, than they owe me; and if through dear Aunt Clare I can do a little, even in the most material way, to redress the balance I shall be happier in myself and—who knows?—my art may find a new direction, less resentful, less chaotic, less hostile—less contrary (if I may put it so) to what I should *like* to feel.'

At that point he again reverted to his desire to *give*. 'I'm forty-five, a year older than you, and at this time of day I can't change my nature. But I should like to devote the rest of my few and evil days to *giving*—and that is where Aunt Clare comes in. She gave to institutions, to societies, to charities, to hospitals—she had a whole budget of impersonal disbursements which varied little in extent from year to year. No doubt she did a great deal of good, but I doubt if she got much pleasure from it, or much credit either. People said she was mean, as she sometimes was, in small ways; she had no wish to appear rich, and any form of publicity was hateful to her. But as you know, it was thanks to her that from being a struggling composer I became a non-struggling one. She made this "accommodation" for me in a rather chilly way, I remember. I was standing under the domed skylight in her hall just after luncheon, and she said, rather shyly, "You will be hearing from my solicitors, Gilbert, and I hope the news will be as satisfactory to you as it is to me." at wasn't a large sum she settled on me, it had been calculated to I nicety to keep me equally from poverty and affluence—she knew what my nature was like, how responsive I am (or used to be) to responsibility, and how quickly I tire of it when the responsibility (for whatever reason) seems to wear off.

'I love myself, don't you? At least not myself, for I often dislike myself, but I love my self-hood. It seems such a waste, that this should vanish, as soon it must. "Je me regrette"—as someone said. I often wish I could find some young person to take on my life where I left it off. To bequeath oneself—just as Aunt Clare, 'poor' Clare, bequeathed her money! I do hope she has got some feeling of personal survival out of it. She had no children, of course—nor have I, as far as I know, being a bachelor; but children are not necessarily a passport to immortality, or even to happiness in this world. But who, what young man or what young woman for that matter, would want to take over one's life, which would involve, I suppose, taking over one's personality? They might find the change so distasteful that they would commit suicide the next day!

'However, my aunt's possessions are an extension of myself in time to come, just as they were an extension of herself in her time. When I think of her, I think of them—the pictures on the grey-green walls on to which the sunshine (if any) was admitted so reluctantly, and it all seems to make a synthesis of *something*, but Heaven knows what! She wasn't really happy, but who is?

'This letter is inexcusably long, and I don't remember what I have said or not said. The Death Duty people are much slower than death, and not everything my aunt left me has yet come to hand, but you *will* accept the little Girtin, won't you? The colours, though they make a contrast, don't really *quarrel*. Please take it, dear Edward, I should be grateful if you did, and so I'm sure would the shade of 'poor' Clare, who had, in a way, so little to worry about, and yet so much.

Yours ever,
Gilbert.'

Chapter Two

I AT once wrote to Gilbert a letter of quite fulsome thanks to say how overjoyed I should be to have the Girtin, he was one of my favourite painters (which is quite true) and a great deal more in that vein. When the picture arrived I wrote again. 'I am more than grateful to you,' I said, 'for your fantastic generosity. Would you be free to dine on Tuesday or Wednesday or Thursday of next week?' He wrote back after a day or two, saying to my surprise (for he was not a man of many engagements) that, alas, he wouldn't be free. I wrote again, and telephoned again, dilating on my gratitude and my admiration for the picture, but no, there was always some obstacle.

*

It was from Eileen Faulkner that I next had news—as opposed to the lack of news which had been a feature (if a lack can be a feature) of my telephone-talks with Gilbert.

I was never sure that Eileen approved of me or even liked me, but sometimes she asked me to a meal and I enjoyed her company and the company of her husband, Adrian, who was a tough man, engaged in some business or businesses. He did not belong to my world, but he was tolerant of me and I of him. After a time the conversation turned to Gilbert.

'I haven't heard from him for an age,' I said.

Eileen raised her eyebrows.

'But I thought he was one of your closest friends.'

'He was,' I replied, 'and I suppose he still is. He gave me his aunt's lovely Girtin, but since then—'

'I expect he has been very busy,' Eileen interposed, 'distributing her treasures. To a man of his sensitive temperament—'

'Poor old Clare was a sensible, hard-headed woman,' Adrian said. 'I wouldn't know how sensitive she was. But if you, Eileen, had ever shown an intelligent interest in the arts, as Edward has— well, it's his job—then she might have left you one of her Titians or Rembrandts.'

'No,' I protested. 'Never. She would have left them to Gilbert, if she had any pictures of that quality, which I doubt. She would have left them to Gilbert. Whatever people may say, I'm convinced she didn't ear-mark anything for anyone, except Gilbert.'

'What about some institution or other,' suggested Adrian, 'or perhaps the Church? She was always a good church-woman. The only time I met her (how badly you played your cards then, Eileen) I thought she might have had a vocation for religion.'

'So as not to be mistaken for a Jewess,' said Eileen, tartly. 'No, I take that back. She was no more a Jewess than her husband was a Jew. How odd it is to think that they were once beneath us socially (if that is possible!). And then when he made his pile out of whatever it was,—something slightly shady—which he did in an incredibly short space of time, they were wafted into spheres far, far above ours, and mixed with people in the same income bracket with themselves. I don't know if they ever quite made the grade, socially, I mean. If not, it may have accounted for Lady Ditchworth's stiffness, poker-back and poker-face—'

'I can never think of her as Lady Ditchworth,' interrupted Adrian. 'I always think of her as Aunt Clare.'

'Of course, he was knighted shortly before he died. I don't think she cared for the title, or the name. After his death heaps of people wanted to manage her fortune for her, but she kept them at bay, all except Gilbert.'

'I'm sure Gilbert never wanted to manage her fortune for her,' I said, warmly. 'A fortune-hunter is the last thing he has ever been.'

Eileen agreed.

'No, and perhaps that's why she was fond of him.'

'Could one be fond of a man just because he wasn't a fortune-hunter?' I asked idly.

Eileen considered.

'I suppose it would depend on how many fortune-hunters there were about. Penelope stayed true to Ulysses in spite of all the suitors. They were fortune-hunters, but he wasn't.'

'Do we know that he wasn't? I asked. 'Ithaca was a considerable property, and she kept it warm for him. But no one has ever suggested that Gilbert—'

'Please, please, Edward,' Eileen held up a warning hand.

'I only meant,' I said reprovingly, 'that at least half of the good music in the world has been due to the generosity of patrons and patronesses. Should we have had the Brandenburg Concertos, or the Razumovsky Quartets, or the Waldstein Sonata—or the—'

'Does it matter? The point is that his Aunt Clare believed in him, and but for her he wouldn't have got anywhere. And now Aunt Clare Ditchworth has made it possible for Gilbert to realize his ambitions—even if it means hiring the Festival Hall!'

Adrian broke in:

'Really, Eileen, you must stop talking like this, or we shall think you are jealous of Gilbert.'

'I don't want his mouldy old pictures,' Eileen said, 'or the other objects that keep seeping into him when the executors release them. Much good may they do him. I'm glad I'm not one.'

'Do you mean an object, or an executor?' Adrian asked.

When she didn't answer, I said what had been in my mind all along:

'But I wish I could hear from Gilbert. We were such good friends, but since he gave me the Girtin water-colour, I've lost touch with him. It's not for want of thanking him, I've exhausted the vocabulary of gratitude.'

'Perhaps you've overdone it,' Adrian said, dryly.

'Oh no, how could I?'

Suddenly I felt irritated with the whole situation, and Gilbert's lack of response to my response.

'I haven't seen your Girtin,' said Eileen, rather as if I had deliberately hidden it, 'and I know very little about pictures, but it may be too representational for modern taste. I mean, it may depict whatever it is *as* it is. I expect he meant it for an insult, he knew it was the kind of painting you liked, and practised, so he gave it to you just to show you up as a square. He meant it to be a smear, an oblique kind of smear, as they say nowadays.'

Her husband took her up.

'What nonsense, Eileen. Of course there are masses of people who would be glad to have a Girtin, much more than they would to have a Paul Klee or a Rouault, or one of those pictures that looks like something else. Edward needn't be ashamed of giving houseroom to a Girtin, and if he is, he can easily dispose of it. Have you thought of selling it, Edward? I should, if I were you.'

A silence fell.

'I hadn't really,' I said, 'though it would be a solution, if Gilbert's wonderful gift has come between him and me. I value his friendship much more than his picture, supposing I have to choose between them.'

'Oh, not to worry,' Eileen said. 'I expect you've got it all wrong. Just because you haven't seen him for a week or two—'

'A month or two,' I corrected her.

'Well, then, a month or two. What is the difference? It doesn't mean that he has cast you off. Besides, you were never all that fond of him, you liked his friend Myra better—'

I made no comment on this.

'I don't know him well,' went on Eileen, 'but I've known him a long time, and his character and his behaviour are full of surprises, though you wouldn't think so, to look at him. That wary, rodent-like appearance, in spite of his round face and snub nose, as if there was always a cat round the corner! Though why a cat should be interested in him in *that* way—to catch him, I mean,—perhaps only Myra or Barbara could explain. But then I'm not a cat.'

Neither Adrian nor I denied this, and Eileen continued:

'Would you believe it, in the past, before he got this—this high-class junk from Aunt Clare, he used to give *us* things—nothing special—but I seem to remember that he never liked me

15

better after these mementoes, it took him some time to recover from the effort of giving. He moved towards generosity and then away from it, if you know what I mean, like a mouse who has given away a bit of cheese to another mouse, (suppose they do share it among themselves) and then regrets it.'

'Really, Eileen,' Adrian interposed, 'anyone who heard you might think you were jealous of Edward.'

'I'm not jealous of him,' retorted Eileen. 'I may be a little envious. I was only trying to explain Gilbert to you and Edward, who don't seem to understand him. I expect he is tormented thinking how he should dispose of his aunt's largesse, and *who* is to have *what*. And there is nothing so disturbing (so people have told me, Edward) nothing that puts one on such bad terms with oneself, as well as the people who are hoping to benefit, as trying to distribute one's ill-gotten gains.'

She paused for breath, and Adrian said with mock severity, 'Eileen, you should take that back. Alfred Ditchworth's gains may have been ill-gotten, but Gilbert's weren't.'

'I know, I know,' said Eileen. 'I'm sure he was fond of the old girl, and he was her nephew and her only blood relation except her sister with whom she was not on speaking terms, still less on giving terms—why, we don't know, unless the story is true that the sister whose name we all forget, said something uncomplimentary about Alfred Ditchworth. "Who are you to talk?" Aunt Clare is supposed to have said. "None of your four husbands was as honest as my one," and she cut her out of her Will.'

'But she left Gilbert in it,' Adrian said.

'Yes, because he hung around her and made up to her, and didn't keep up with her sister, his mother, from whom he was *at least* three step-fathers removed. No, I'm not criticizing him,' she went on, glancing at Adrian and me. '*We* have nothing to distribute except to our children, and very little to them, precious as they are. Gilbert, poor dear, means well, but he suffers from a divided mind, that's why his music is so ear-splitting, and when he thinks about dividing the spoil—should Electra Motherwell have this, or Anthony Peasbottom have that,—he gets into a panic. But when he's *settled* something (I don't mean estate-wise!) and got it off his chest, he will settle down, too. It will just be a problem that his conscience has solved, and though *we* don't come into it, you and I, Adrian, (why should we, we aren't nephews or nieces of Lady Ditchworth) we shall all be friends again.'

Chapter Three

I DIDN'T again ask Gilbert to meet me, not because I was offended or hurt, although I was; I just felt, as was all too plain, that he didn't want to see me, and that was that.

'What have I *done*?' I asked myself, a question that must have occurred to many people when someone, for no apparent reason, has dropped them. Have I shown too little, or too much gratitude? Have I been ham-fisted, in some way?

It was most mysterious. Loan oft loseth both itself and friend, but surely that is not true of a gift? A gift enriches him that gives and him that takes. The recipient of a gift may take umbrage (as well as the gift) and feel he should have had more, or less, or everything or nothing, anything but that particular thing,—these objections are frivolous and captious, but they do sometimes happen with spoilt, touchy people, or people who want one to feel small. I have sometimes had a gift handed back to me, with 'Oh please, don't give me *that*! I haven't room for it!' or, 'It might get broken,' or 'I've got dozens like it, anyway!' There is no surer way of deflating someone than by looking his gift-horse in the mouth. Ingratitude is an indignity as well as a wound.

I was beginning to persuade myself that Gilbert had been ungrateful to me, not I to him, when the telephone buzzed. I was so thankful to be relieved from the vexation of my own thoughts that I rushed to the instrument and smiled into it inanely, as if it had been a long-lost friend.

'Hullo!'

'Hullo!'

I was never good at recognizing voices on the telephone. A sudden thought, a sudden hope crossed my mind, releasing all sorts of pent-up feelings.

'Gilbert?'

'No, no, I expect the wish was father to the thought. It's Adrian.'

'Adrian!' I exclaimed, concealing, I hoped, my disappointment. 'How wonderful! But I didn't recognize your voice. Have you had it *lifted*?'

Adrian laughed.

'Well, I have in a way. Not permanently, though. It will soon revert to its *basso profondo*. But I am excited, I have to admit.'

'Is it anything to do with your gambling activities?'

'No.' Adrian sounded much more like himself, much less cocky. He had once had beginner's luck as a gambler, and had then spent half his life trying to recover it, in vain. 'All the same,' —and his voice again went up a tone or two, 'I have been lucky, and Eileen and I wanted to celebrate. Would you be free to-morrow night? It's very short notice, but the luck has been at short notice,—I suppose luck always is. I'm not going to tell you now, but you'll have a surprise, perhaps two surprises.'

*

I had to be content with that, and with looking forward to the following evening. As one grows older, one becomes less capable of surprise, or at any rate of pleasant surprises. All the same I couldn't help wondering what Adrian had up his sleeve. Not one surprise, but two, almost as many as the Heathen Chinee.

Meanwhile, I had the Girtin to look at. I had, if truth be told, been a little disappointed with it at first, because it was a townscape, not a landscape. It was a long, thin picture, painted in Paris, which the painter visited in the last two years of his tragically short life, and it was a picture of Paris painted from the left bank of the Seine, which was much wider and calmer than I remembered it, so wide and so calm, so utterly lake-like, that the buildings on the further shore were reflected as if in a looking-glass. In the reflection they were more simplified, and oddly enough more solid, than were their originals on the bank above. It seemed as though the artist had been more interested in the images that the buildings mirrored in the smooth grey-green waters, than in the buildings themselves.

I felt there might be a moral to this, for are we not all more interested in the 'image' of whoever, or whatever it may be, than in the person or the thing itself?

The figure of Gilbert, for instance, how fascinating it would have been to detect the differences, if it had been reflected in the waters of the Seine. But the Seine would have had to be as unruffled as it was, presumably, in Girtin's time; no traffic plying to and fro, no *Belle Jardinière* (how well I remembered that antique, picturesque steamer, hooting its warnings as it went by, and leaving its trail of foam).

But Girtin had not been content with a study in likenesses, however carefully differentiated. Above the river-bank, and far into the skies, soared the dream Dome of the Pantheon, a mile or so away, sunlit between sunlit clouds; and the dome was not reflected in the river; it stood by itself. The whole composition centred round it and looked up to it; it did not need, it would not suffer, the emphasis of duplication.

I moved the painting this way and that, I did a lot of im-promptu picture-hanging, but put it where I would, still it proclaimed its independence, its refusal to submit to the role of a picture among pictures, a property-picture humbly shadowing forth Girtin's art. Two or three times I unhooked the canvas, trying to put it on good terms with the others, but it insisted on taking pride of place, and in the end I hung it in my bedroom, where it was safe from competition.

It was clear that although I liked the picture and welcomed it not only for its own sake but for what it meant in the way of friendship and gratitude to Gilbert, and more distantly to his Aunt Clare, it was equally clear that it didn't like *me*, and wanted me to know it. It wouldn't fit into any scheme I had prepared for it. And why should a painting by Girtin so demean itself? It was presumptuous to think I could incorporate it with my own feeble efforts or with the less feeble efforts of painters whose work I had collected through the years. It stuck out like a sore thumb.

*

The disturbing intruder disposed of, I returned to the familiar scene. I wasn't ashamed of choosing it again for, to compare small things with great (as most artists have to) how often did Cézanne paint Mt. St. Victoire? The *voyage autour de ma chambre* presented a much more restricted prospect, but it had furnished me with many subjects even if, *au fond,* they were the same subject.

So I sat down to my task, and my enjoyment of it, relieved, as I thought, and full of hope; but I couldn't have made a bigger mistake. I did not expect, I did not wish the familiar objects round me to repeat themselves, or their images, to my pictorial eye (if I had one). I hoped for, indeed I relied on, capturing certain gradations of emphasis, certain modulations of key which are the secret of variations on a theme,—so divine in Schubert's music.

But they did not come to my aid—these shades of difference whose difference, in the end, creates a new harmony, with an identity of its own.

Instead, they quarelled with each other, and forms and colours which had always been friendly—but not *too* friendly—now seemed at open war, indignant at their enforced juxtaposition. Nothing went with anything else. The sofa would not agree with the carpet; the chairs looked as if they hated each other and belonged to periods (as in fact they did) that had outgrown the past without looking forward to the future. And as for the pictures, which I had chosen for some common quality (I could not have said what) they were like guests at a party, ill-matched and ill-met, who had been formally and correctly introduced, but who would not speak to each other or to me, their host.

Although I knew it was my fault—a failure of imaginative synthesis—I couldn't help feeling that they were to blame. They didn't like the Girtin coming between them, even though it was banished to my bedroom. Being jealous of it they were jealous of each other, for jealousy so quickly spreads.

Very well, I thought; have it your own way, I will paint you like a coven of Kilkenny cats, each bent on destroying the other, and the picture will be like Gilbert's music, a concatenation of cacophonies, unrelated and unresolved.

But I had as little gift for discord as Gilbert had for harmony. My nature was against it, and I felt like a naturally pacific person, forced into a quarrel. One's creative faculty is part of one's temperament, sometimes only a small part, and not always in tune with it, but inseparable from the whole. Gilbert was the most peaceable of men, yet his gift, applauded by some, expressed the hostile reactions of a fighting-cock.

Outwardly he was inoffensive and retiring. Short and slight in stature with straight fair hair, not a silver thread in them, a fresh complexion which made him look younger than his years, and mild blue eyes so diffident that they seldom met one's own. A mouse-like appearance and personality, as Eileen said; but within it lurked those hidden fires that expressed themselves in music with the irresponsible fury of a major conflagration.

How different from me! I knew my own appearance well, as every artist must who has essayed to paint his self-portrait. The mirror could not tell me what other people saw, nor what the camera saw, which was sometimes disconcerting,—but essentially it was the same appearance. I was tall, swarthy, rangy, mustachioed, with a black felt hat to match. I might have passed for a brigand or a cow-boy. Myra, in times gone by, had called me both. Yet now it seemed as if she preferred Gilbert's innocuous, undistinguished looks. Women are unpredictable.

But did she? He hadn't given her a present, as far as we knew, and yet unlike us, she was (so the rumour went) still bidden to his board, and possibly even to his bed. In old days the entertainment he offered at mealtimes was so meagre that it became a by-word,—Gilbert without Sullivan, someone called it. But since his aunt's death he might have engaged a *cordon bleu* and the feasts would be Lucullan instead of Barmecide.

I began to feel a grievance against Gilbert, who by his uncalled for, unseasonable gift, had put me in a jam. He has done it on purpose, I told myself; he knows how suggestible I am, and by giving me the Girtin, which so far surpasses my own timid efforts he has also given me an inferiority complex, from which I shall not recover.

'*Quidquid id est, timeo Danaos et dona ferentes.*'

I had never thought of Gilbert as taking part in the siege of Troy and deluding its defenders with the ruse of the wooden horse, but it was a myth as old as humanity. The Girtin was the horse, chockfull of demons, all intent on destroying the belief in their own powers by which all artists live.

I thought again, and yet again. Obviously it was untrue that Gilbert wanted to harm me. His gift was meant to give me pleasure, not to make me distrust my own gifts, such as they were. One's prejudices, even one's wayward thoughts, are stronger far than reason in determining one's state of mind. Gradually I began to do Gilbert justice. But what of Aunt Clare? Might she not from the grave be exerting a sinister influence? Who knew what effect her un-ideal husband, her childlessness, her possible conviction of having given more to causes and people than she had got in return, might have had on her?

Only Gilbert knew what she was really like—if he did know.

Sadly the minutes passed. I stared at my canvas covered with warring objects, which every minute grew more distasteful to me. Then I arose and tried to tear it up, and when I found I wasn't strong enough, I dismembered it with my palette knife, as a murderer might.

Later I calmed down, and told myself, all this has nothing to do with the picture. It's because Gilbert used to be my friend, and now isn't. The others feel it too, the others whom Gilbert has enriched out of his aunt's legacy. They have the boodle but they miss the friendship, just as I do, but not as much, because I am, or was, a greater friend of his than they were, except perhaps for. . . .

23

I did not allow my thoughts to frame the name, but went back to look at the picture housed so unworthily in my bedroom. How beautiful it was, basking in what someone called 'Girtin's incomparable serenity of mood'!

Chapter Four

I WAS still meditating on gratitude and ingratitude and wondering which was the greater threat to human happiness, when I arrived at Adrian's flat. Even the door had a new look; the brass letter-box shone almost aggressively, as if it had lately received good tidings. A delicious whiff of impending dinner accompanied Adrian as he opened the door.

'Now you must tell me,' I said, as we sat down. The sitting-room-cum-dining-room, often as it was done up, always slightly jarred on me, because the pictures were meant to go with the room, not the other way round. There was one of mine, over the fireplace, but I felt it was in bad company.

I could hear Eileen's quick footsteps in the kitchen, the pregnant pauses followed by bursts of anxious activity.

'You must tell me,' I repeated.

But Adrian didn't want to. 'I'll wait until you have had a drink,' he said, 'or the shock may be too great. Anyway Eileen must be with us when we break the news. We don't always agree but we do agree about this. She pretends not to be excited, but she is really and I should hate her to miss your expression of stupefaction. I know you always think I'm slightly batty, but if I told you now you'd think I had definitely crossed the lunatic fringe.'

I sat down with my dry martini, and containing my impatience, stared out of the window with its pleasant view of trees and garden. Pleasant but uninspiring. I knew it by heart. Adrian followed my eyes.

'They are getting things into some sort of shape here now,' he said carelessly. 'After the war it was awful, it was a shambles! Such people, coming from everywhere, and nowhere, and mostly black. I don't want to sound snobbish, but really what they did, and didn't do! I was told that even the rats avoided the district—'

'Well, that's good news,' I said, 'but I don't suppose it is the good news you were going to tell me.'

'Well, no,' he said, 'but they are connected in a sort of way. We think of leaving this rather suburban area, and moving nearer to the heart of London, if you see what I mean.'

'I'm glad, Adrian, if you're glad.' In this mood I couldn't connect him with the Adrian I knew.

'Oh yes, I'm glad, and Eileen is glad, too. The buses, and all those chores! Poor girl, she's had a rough time and I shall be so much nearer to my job. You haven't a job, so it wouldn't affect you.'

'Well, I have, Adrian, as a matter of fact.'

'Yes, but not a real job, not a commuter's job. Don't be offended, but you just sit on your backside.'

'What else have I to sit on? What do you sit on?'

'Oh on nothing, I'm just a strap-hanger, I rest on air. *Mais nous devons changer tout cela*. Eileen!' he called, 'where is the champagne?'

Eileen appeared in a very smart apron. Having kissed me she said to her husband, 'I thought the champagne was your department. But perhaps you will open the bottle while I make myself decent for Edward.'

'And not for me?' he asked.

'You don't want me to be decent.'

'I don't mind if you are this once,' and he followed her into the kitchen, whence he emerged bringing the champagne in an ice-bucket improvised out of a metal waste-paper basket.

For a time he wrestled with the cork. 'Give it to me,' I urged. 'No cork has ever got the better of me.'

'No,' he said, 'you are too professional. I want to hear the report, and then see the cork hit the ceiling and if possible go through it. I want it to do a *lot* of damage.'

'You might be describing Gilbert's music.'

'Perhaps I am,' Adrian answered darkly, his fingers still

26

struggling with the knob and wires of the cork, his eyes closed, his mouth twice its ordinary length, his teeth clenched, his forehead so corrugated with effort that he looked quite unlike himself.

'You'll burst a blood-vessel,' I exclaimed.

At that moment, Eileen came in, prettier and happier and better-dressed than I had ever seen her, to be greeted with a terrific bang, and a sense of something invisibly whizzing. She closed her eyes and put her hands over her ears.

'Where has it gone?' she asked at last. 'I hope it hasn't done any damage. Be quick, Adrian, the champagne is all coming out.'

He hadn't reckoned with this, and the carpet got its libation before the glasses got theirs.

'Oh dear, oh dear, it's all because we never *have* champagne.'

When the cork had been retrieved from the far end of the room, the bottle, still fuming and foaming like an angry geni, had been confined to its waste-paper basket, and the food was on the table, Adrian said, almost tragically:

'He doesn't realize that this is a celebration, Eileen.'

'I thought it must be, Adrian. But for what, and in honour of whom?'

'I'll take your second question first,' said Adrian, 'In honour of you, of course, and someone else, who we hoped would make a fourth. But at the last moment he couldn't come.'

'I don't mind,' I said. 'For me three's company. But who is the shadowy fourth—?'

'He's not all that shadowy,' said Eileen, 'and certainly not shady. He's a great darling, and if I ever called him anything else, forget it.'

'Forget it,' repeated Adrian, solemnly. 'But first, guess what the celebration's for?'

'You've won something on a race?'

'Wrong. Actually, I've lost something.'

'Well then, the football pools?'

'Really, Edward, as if I—'

'I know how fond you are of gambling,' I grumbled. 'You

needn't hide it from me, I don't disapprove of it. Perhaps it was something to do with what they call Ernie—'

'No, it wasn't,' Adrian snapped. 'You have a one-track mind. You see me in terms of betting, instead of the long-suffering, sober businessman that I am. Have another guess. Just look round the room.'

I didn't want to, for I know how quickly one's face registers disapproval.

'Well, there's the champagne bottle.'

'Yes, but look again.'

Reluctantly I swivelled my eyes round. So much *not* to look at! And then, at the back of my head, in a space obviously cleared for it, I saw something that astonished me.

'Oh, what a lovely picture! Is it a Vuillard?'

'You're right,' said Adrian. 'Get up and have a look at it.'

I did so. It was summer-time, if not summer weather, the curtains hadn't been drawn, or the candles lit: I could still see the picture by daylight. Unlike many of his pictures, it was an out-of-door scene, a mother and her child plunging forward into sunshine that irradiated the room and almost dazzled me. And indeed it must have dazzled them, the rough-clad peasant woman and her little daughter who were stumbling, clutching each other's hands, almost blinded by the glow, into a furnace of light which, one felt, might almost burn them up. The light was on the cottage and the trees behind them, and on the cornfield in front of them. It drenched the picture, with an indescribable effect of joy, but most vividly was it to be seen in the two faces, replicas of each other, which seemed to give it out as well as to receive it.

How glorious, to tumble into the future, with all that confidence!

*

'Guess how we came by it,' asked Adrian.

I knew the answer, but it is always disappointing to a questioner, however frivolous, if one isn't mystified.

'You stole it?'

28

'No.'

'You found it under an elderberry bush in Dulwich?'

'No.'

'You bought it?'

'No, a thousand times no.'

'Was it a present?'

'Yes! Yes!' They clapped their hands and looked at me expectantly, no doubt wanting me to ask them whose.

I have never seen two people more transformed, not only in attitude to life but even in physical appearance, than were Eileen and Adrian since I saw them last. Adrian was far less saturnine and Eileen was positively radiant.

'Was it anyone I know?' I asked.

'Oh yes,' said Eileen, 'you know him very well.'

'Do I like him?'

Eileen and Adrian exchanged glances.

'Certainly,' said Adrian, 'he's an old chum of yours.'

'Do you like him?' I pursued.

'Oh yes,' said Eileen fervently. 'He's our great, our *greatest* friend.'

I remembered how Eileen had talked about Gilbert, the last time we met.

'A friend of long standing?'

'Yes, years and years.'

'Not the shadowy fourth you were expecting for dinner?'

Again Eileen and Adrian flashed a signal to each other, and Adrian said, 'As a matter of fact he was. Gilbert you mean, don't you?'

I nodded.

'He has always been a special friend of ours,' said Adrian firmly. 'But all the same it was a great surprise, as well as a great pleasure —we have thanked him, of course. And we hoped he would be here, to be thanked again. But someone got in first.'

'What do you think the picture is worth?' I asked.

It wasn't altogether an innocent question. The Girtin had been in my mind from the beginning. It was more to my taste than the Vuillard, but in the saleroom! Feelings came over me, unworthy feelings, that I tried to suppress. Were my looks green with envy? I hoped not.

'When I said "worth",' I hastily amended, 'I meant worth in terms of happiness, glory, exuberance, enhancement of life, provision for the enjoyment of your future years. A thing of beauty is a joy for ever—'

'Oh,' said Adrian, 'it's a very nice picture, a bit old-fashioned, and not really right in this room, is it? It doesn't go with modern things. We don't mean to *keep* it. When you asked what it was worth, I thought you meant saleswise. What did the valuer tell us, Eileen? You're the financial expert.'

'He said about £10,000,' said Eileen promptly, 'might be more, might be less. Being a gift, it's free of Income Tax. At least we hope so. As to Capital Gains, we don't know yet, it's something that even the experts don't understand.'

'But you definitely mean to part with the picture?'

'Of course,' they both said at once. 'Otherwise,' added Eileen, 'why did Gilbert give it us?'

There seemed so many answers to this question. At last I said: 'So Gilbert was to have been here tonight?'

Eileen pointed to his place already laid. 'He telephoned at the last minute to say he couldn't make it,' Adrian took her up. 'He was particularly sorry to miss you. But there is a chance of seeing him tonight, if you feel up to it. The Dankervilles are giving a party—it's for him, really,—and he may turn up for it. It's quite informal, but they asked us to come, and bring you with us.'

'The Dankervilles?' I said. 'But what have they to do with Gilbert?'

'Oh, they once helped him over a bad patch, and he is grateful to them,' Adrian said. 'At any rate he gave them something, a horse, I think. If you would like to come along, do. Of course, he may not be there.'

*

But Gilbert was there. I saw him across the room. I was talking to Antonia and Henry Dankerville, in that brief moment that a host and hostess allow themselves to greet a guest.

'How good of you to ask me.'

'How good of you to come.'

'Now that we've said that,' said Antonia, 'let me show you the picture. It's *there*—forgive me for pointing—just over Gilbert's head.'

'The picture?'

'Oh, I forgot you didn't know. The picture Gilbert has given us, in memory of his Aunt Clare. We thought we'd ask a few friends in to see it, and him.'

'It's a damn good picture,' said her husband. 'I like it quite a lot. You're in that line of business, Edward, can you guess who painted it?'

I stared across the many heads, bowed over their drinks, or upright, contemplating them. One or two faces, invisible to me, were turned towards the picture. Clouds of smoke intervened. I tried to study it.

'You see it's a horse, Edward?'

'Yes, Henry.'

'And what I like about it is that it's *like* a horse. And the girl with the black velvet cap who's riding is *like* a girl.'

'Certainly.'

'Some pictures you see nowadays, you wouldn't know which was the horse and which the girl, ha ha.'

Again I agreed.

'And I like all that light and air, if you know what I mean, and the feeling of the Downs, where they're going to have a jolly good ride. Especially the horse.'

'Why especially the horse?'

'I mean I like the horse better. Antonia never really liked horses, did you?'

He turned to her, but she was busy with another guest.

'But go and have a look at it, old boy.'

'I will, but I never was a judge of horse-flesh, Henry.'

'No, but you're a judge of pictures. I know that artists have painted other things as well—girls, for instance!—but quite a lot have painted horses. When you've had a drink, go and look at it, old boy.'

I sped a parting shaft.

'What will you do with it?'

'Do with it?' Henry repeated. 'What does one do with a picture? Look at it, I suppose—and then, when I get too old to ride, I shall remember what it felt like.'

*

Threading my way through the throng I met Myra.

'Dear Myra! Fancy meeting you here, with our horse-coping friend!'

'And fancy meeting you!' said Myra. 'To think that wild horses should drag us together!'

'They couldn't drag us apart!' I said.

She smiled up at me, she had to look up, though she was only three inches shorter than I was. Now in her middle forties, she had soft brown eyes in an oval face, with soft brown hair to match, over a rather high forehead. Her nose was short and her mouth rather full; I don't remember what she wore; I believe it was a long, lavender-coloured silk dress with flounces. But I always looked at her face first, and last. And yet her voice was the greatest of her attractions for me; it was low and seemed to come from a small place, without much range of over-tone and undertone, but with such a purity of quality! My mind's ear could remember it even when my mind's eye which is treacherous (even in a would-be painter) could not recall her face.

'I didn't know that Gilbert was such a great friend of the Dankerville's.'

'I don't think he is,' Myra answered. 'Perhaps that's why he's here.'

'What do you mean by that enigmatic remark?'

'I mean,' . . . When Myra hesitated, the flute-note stopped dead: it did not prolong its tone as a violin does.

32

'I don't think he sees many people now,' she said.

'Why not? He never was a gadabout, but he used to like to see his friends.'

Myra looked distressed. 'You mean you haven't seen him?' I ignored this.

'He is our benefactor,' she went on.

'Certainly he's mine, maybe he is yours,—'

'Oh yes, he has been a benefactor to me.' She didn't say what kind of benefactor.

'But as much a benefactor as you have been a benefactress?' I asked.

Myra turned away and said, doubtfully, 'I don't think you can weigh human relationships against each other in that cutlet-for-cutlet fashion. Shall we go and look at the Munnings?—It is a Munnings, isn't it?'

'Oh yes,' I said, 'and one of his best.'

When a little group of admirers had moved away from the picture, we were able to study it close to. Henry Dankerville had described it well, the sunny Downs, the horse (a dapple-grey) and the girl astride it, with the morning sunshine, the sunshine of the promise of life, lighting up her face.

'Beautiful,' I said, and couldn't repress a catch in my voice. 'And Henry likes it—more as the portrait of a horse than as a picture, perhaps. How lucky he is, in more ways than one.'

'How else is he lucky?'

'Because Gilbert still wants to see him, or consents to see him. Evidently, Myra, a horse is the passport to Gilbert's affections. Shall I give him one? Perhaps you have given him a *stud*.'

Myra showed embarrassment. 'Oh, he's within hailing distance. Do go and talk to him, Edward.'

She drifted away.

*

'Ah, the hero of the hour,' I said. 'We are all singing your praises, Gilbert, I've begun to think of you as a painter, not a composer. The Vuillard, this lovely Munnings, and of course

my Girtin—it's given a new significance to the word "my"—
I've never felt so proprietorial.'

I looked down at Gilbert, and he looked up at me—greenish
eyes, snub nose, smooth, tow-coloured hair,—not at all like a
rodent. But who can describe in words a face that tallies with the
face one knows?

'You like the Munnings?' he said. 'I'm so glad, and I'm so
glad that Henry likes it, too. Between ourselves, he's not one of
my closest friends, but he once did me a very good turn for which
I was—I am—most grateful. This picture,'—he waved towards
it—'was a favourite of Aunt Clare's, though I don't suppose she
was much of a horsewoman. But perhaps she liked to think of
herself riding into the sunrise—that bright light from the east,
washed with pale gold, very unlike the gold that Uncle Alfred
gave her.'

'Oh, do you think so *very* unlike, Gilbert?'

'As different as chalk from cheese. How *can* you compare
them, that liquid primrose glow in the sky, with its presage of
youth, and that dull, heavy smoulder of real gold—invisible
unless you turned the lights on—in the banker's vaults where
Uncle Alfred kept it? Oh, I know he didn't keep it there, but the
two ideas, derived from one word, one colour, *could* they be more
unlike?'

Gilbert's voice rose almost as a squeak, and a mottled red
mantled his cheeks. 'If I were to write a "Golden Sonata",—and
I could, or I could have once—'

'Why can't you now?' I asked. 'I don't feel the unlikeness
between the two kinds of gold. After all, they both are manifestations of Nature, even if one is atmospheric and the other
mineral—'

'It's like comparing a candle with a searchlight,' Gilbert said,
almost violently.

'Which is which?'

'Oh, Edward, it depends on how you look at it.'

'I don't think it does,' I argued. 'Surely you can decide, which
is the candle and which the searchlight? In any case, I don't

34

think they are incompatible. I can imagine them mingling in the same picture, so why not in a golden sonata?'

'Because, dear Edward, certain things, and certain ideas, are basically opposed,—good and evil, black and white, war and peace. I used to feel they were, as well as know they were—but somehow, since Aunt Clare died, and left me these things to hand out—'

'But *did* she leave them to you to hand out?'

'Oh, that's another story—her spirit and mine are still debating it. What she bequeathed me amounted to a passport to reconciliation. Well, I've used it, or some of it, as I think she would have wished me to, for her sake and for mine. But the upshot is, I don't seem able to compose any more on the old lines, and I'm too old, myself, to find new ones, based on reciprocity. So I've kept in reserve one or two outlets for—'

'For what, Gilbert?'

'Oh, how can I put it? For *otherness,* I suppose; for relationships which haven't been undermined and contaminated by gifts. Relationships in which any hostility that *I* feel—don't *you* feel hostile, Edward, from time to time?—can be freely countered by the hostility that *they* feel,—without them owing *me* anything, or *me* owing them anything.'

'What a gloomy view of life you take,' I said. 'Is your hostility really *necessary*? I've managed to get on with only a moderate amount of it—but of course one *is* provoked, sometimes.'

Gilbert's face became more than ever cherubic.

'Always, I think,' he said, '*always.* What work of art, my dear Edward, except yours and . . . and Girtin's, hasn't been inspired by provocation?'

'Does provocation mean contrast?'

'To me it does,' said Gilbert, 'and what's more, Edward, to me provocation is the breath of life. Forgive me for saying this, but how could I like you if at the same time I didn't like you?'

I pondered over this.

'I can like you without disliking you,' I said.

'Then you are an exception.' Gilbert looked round the crowded

35

room with the air of a prisoner trying to escape. 'You are an exception and I envy you.'

'I envy *you*, Gilbert,' I retaliated. 'With the help of your dear Aunt Clare, you have been privileged—yes, privileged—to make the lives of several people happy. Not only in a material way, or an aesthetic way' (I didn't say that the Faulkners meant to sell their Vuillard), 'but in the sense that, through you, they are happier, more in tune with the universe, if you like to put it so, than they were before. And doesn't that make *you* feel happier?'

Gilbert looked at me despairingly.

'I'm afraid not. You see, happiness isn't my trade—I only wish it was. Frankly, Edward, I don't believe in it.'

'But my dear Gilbert!—'

'Yes, you may say "my dear Gilbert," but *am* I so dear?'

He had hurt me at last.

'Yes, of course you are.'

'As dear as I was before I gave you the little Girtin?'

'I don't think it made any difference,' I said shortly. 'I was fond of you before and I am fond of you now. If you would like to take the picture back, by all means do so. I like the picture very much, but I like you better.'

Gilbert gave me his most disarming smile.

'Even the gods cannot recall their gifts, can they? Much less I, and still less Aunt Clare, who I hope is in Heaven. But if she thought that by dishing out presents—'

'It's you, Gilbert, who are dishing them out.'

'Well, whoever it is,—if she thought that she was distributing goodness in the form of gifts, she was grievously mistaken. Her namesake, Saint Clare, realized that to do people good, you must exact the utmost sacrifices from them, not try to propitiate them with pictures and chocolates, and so on. Oh no, her nuns had a hell of a time. When they were not immured in their convents and were allowed to go out to do good works, they went barefoot and weren't allowed to speak—except perhaps to say "yes" to some particularly revolting beggar. They were vowed to absolute poverty. Even St. Francis himself thought Saint Clare went too

36

far in the direction of austerity. But what an appeal her "rule" has had for seven centuries of dedicated women! There are still thirteen thousand of them, spread about the world. Only, now they sometimes make wedding-cakes. Would you believe it?'

'But how does your aunt come into this,' I asked, 'except by the accident of her name?'

Gilbert hesitated.

'If she had lived in St. Clare's time,' he said, 'she might have founded an Order. It was much easier to do good in those days than it is in these.'

'Explain,' I said.

'Because in those days goodness was an ideal, not only for saving one's own soul, but for saving the souls of others. Today you can only save their bank-balances which is what Aunt Clare tried to do.'

'Let us give her credit for that, Gilbert.'

'I do, I do. But the spirit of the age, as I feel it, is too strong for her intention: to hell with good intentions! One can only make oneself felt by flouting them.'

'Is that what you are trying to do, Gilbert?'

'I suppose it is, in a way.'

'Other people's good intentions, or yours?'

'Both, I think. I want to be free of obligations, as most people do nowadays.'

'The obligations of friendship, you mean?' Gilbert's face showed that he scented criticism in this.

'Unilateral disarmament.'

'Do you regard friendship as a form of hostility?' I asked.

'Well, it can be. I'm sure you often say to yourself, "Poor old Gilbert, I ought to do something about him!"'

' "Ought," ' I said, 'is a much mis-used word. It brings in a moral element which often isn't really there. You *ought* to write a symphony, or a dysphony—forgive me, Gilbert—or I *ought* to paint a picture. Why *ought* we to?—except for a practical, not a moral reason,—to earn the bread which perisheth. You don't have to—you must be a millionaire, like the Man who broke the

37

Bank at Monte Carlo. No, "ought" doesn't come into it. I *want* to do something about you, as you put it, but you won't let me.'

'Not *let* you, Edward?'

'No, because for some reason you have finished with me. You have paid me off.'

'Edward, I—'

'No, don't contradict me, because it *is* so, as others besides me could tell you. Don't think I am underrating your generosity, because I am not,—I am infinitely grateful to you, as I've told you, time and time again. But for some reason you want to get rid of me.'

'Edward, I—'

'Please let me go on, and understand, Gilbert' (I used his name as if it was an imprecation) 'that I speak for others, as well as for myself. It would be cynical, but it would be quite human, if, having received these gifts, these benefactions, from you, we didn't want to see *you* any more. We have received from you more than we ever expected or deserved—I won't say more than we desired, but there it is—you have done us proud, and we shan't forget it. Goodbye, Gilbert! Cheerio, old boy! Let us meet again in Heaven, if not before!'

I stopped so absorbed with my diagnosis that I didn't even look at him.

Recovering my breath, I went on, 'But *we* aren't like that! We want to see you more than ever, at least,' I added, remembering one or two exceptions, 'most of us do. We were a harmony of kindred souls, weren't we, Gilbert?'

He didn't answer, and a thought suddenly came to me, that I disowned as soon as it came.

'Or perhaps we weren't? Perhaps we represented the discords in your music, and *that* was why—'

'Oh, no, no, no, no, no!'

*

It sounded like a universal negative, as comprehensive, in its small way, as was King Lear's. I realized the emotion behind it,

38

an emotion my temperament couldn't cope with. 'What's the use?' I asked myself, and would have gladly moved away to another, more congenial, topic. But somehow I couldn't.

'And so your art relies on contrasts?' I said at last.

'Oh yes, how else distinguish between what is and what ought to be?'

Suddenly I felt that this was not a suitable subject for a conversation at an evening party, given in Gilbert's honour, where what was, discerned through a tobacco-laden, alcoholic haze, had all the appearance of what *ought* to be. But it seemed to give me an opening.

'I mustn't monopolize you,' I said, 'when so many of your admirers are aching to talk to you. But couldn't we discuss the question of whether art ought to be . . . an idealization or . . . a transcript or an abstraction . . . of life . . . some other time, quite soon?'

'But *is* it a question?' he asked, almost rudely. 'If art isn't a transcript of life,—and that's a wide term, which many people would interpret differently—what is the point of it, what justification has it?'

Warning bells clanged in my mind. 'Steady now, steady!'— but I felt I must stick to my point.

'Somebody said that the Italian painters idealized the human race, or at any rate the human face. Art owes a great deal to the Italian painters, doesn't it? And quite a lot to the Italian composers.'

'Yes, but that's no reason why we should copy it. The architecture of humanism has broken down—it's quite flat. All we have left are the pieces.'

'The jarring atoms, Gilbert?'

'Yes, but isn't it more realistic to recognize them? If we can't agree, let us disagree! . . . What do you think, Barbara?'

Barbara, on Gilbert's other side, couldn't guess why we were laughing and she didn't smile. An interior decorator by profession, she was also Gilbert's friend and secretary; she alone, it was said, could decipher the notation of his music. But for her, his work could never have been performed, still less published. She was the medium between him and his audience, fit though few; and she didn't ask more. She was dark, she was plain, she was unhappy; but a fire burned in her eyes, and that fire was for Gilbert.

'Agree?' she said, 'disagree? I don't know what you are talking about.'

'What I meant to say, Barbara, was that art is an attempt to introduce order into chaos. Life isn't comprehensible, but art *is,* to a certain degree. Trying to imitate life is like trying to imitate chaos. You *have* to impose a pattern on life—every artist has.'

'Are you gunning at me?' asked Gilbert.

'Of course not,' I answered, though I knew I was. 'But if you, Barbara, when you transcribe Gilbert's scores into legible music, which an orchestra, or a quartet, or a pianist can play and make intelligible to an audience,—if, instead of that, you reproduced the squiggles, and let the players hammer away at them at their own sweet will—oh dear, I forget what I was going to say.'

There was a rather chilly pause.

Barbara gave Gilbert an intent look, the significance of which was lost on me.

'When I copy out Gilbert's notation,' she said, slowly, 'I feel I am performing the same service, in a modest way, that Countess Tolstoy did for Tolstoy. She alone could read his script and but for her, *War and Peace* might not have seen the light.'

Not for the first time I wanted to escape from the seriousness of Barbara's outlook, and her uncompromising tongue, although I could not but respect her, for she had dedicated her spare time to Gilbert's work, if not to him.

I saw him detaching himself from his interlocutress of the moment, from me, too, and called out 'Gilbert!' He came back towards us rather unwillingly. I thought he looked like someone who had done many a kindness, and regretted it.

But as he drew near all my old affection for him returned.

'Barbara was boasting,' I said, turning to her accusingly, 'that but for her skill in sight-reading, shall I say? your genius-work wouldn't have assaulted our ears.'

'I said nothing of the sort,' said Barbara.

'Genius-work is much too flattering,' said Gilbert, looking uneasily from Barbara to me, 'and even she can't help me now. I'm in the doldrums, Edward. Has it ever happened to you?'

'I don't aim as high as you do,' I said, glancing at Barbara who obviously agreed, 'and I haven't anyone to inspire me or interpret me. I sit alone with my paint-brush. But couldn't we talk it over, this problem, Gilbert, and try to clarify it?'

He looked away from me.

'When I've got round this next corner—'

'Oh, don't say that, Gilbert. Perhaps I can help you, and you can certainly help me. Tomorrow, for instance.'

'Tomorrow I'm rather tied up, as Barbara knows.'

'Well, the day after, Gilbert—any time by day or night. I insist on seeing you, I really *insist*.' And I glared at him.

'What shall I say, Barbara?' He might almost have been appealing to his nurse.

She shrugged her shoulders.

'Very well, then. Is lunch any good to you?'

'Perfect. At the Rose and Thistle.'

'Which are you?' he said with a return of his old spirit.

'A thistle is what you need,' I answered.

Chapter Five

How quickly one's moods change! When I saw Gilbert's face, a blond moon, peering over the food-bowed heads of the other lunchers at the Rose and Thistle, I didn't want to say anything, except what might give him pleasure.

'Well, here you are!'

'Didn't you think I would be?' said he, defensively.

'Of course I did, but you're such a difficult fish to land.'

'Everything's difficult now.'

'But why, Gilbert? Once I could catch you with a minnow.'

'It's my symphony, I suppose. I don't make any headway with it.'

'I'm sorry to hear that. What's the matter?'

'Oh, it would take too long to explain. A sort of psychological stoppage. The traffic-signals against me. I've sometimes had it before.'

'It's not a change of attitude towards music, is it?' I asked hopefully.

'I suppose it could be,' Gilbert said. 'After Aunt Clare died, and left me all those things—'

'Why didn't you keep them, Gilbert? You were perfectly at liberty to keep them, weren't you?'

When he didn't answer, I said, 'Let's first decide what we are going to eat.'

'Oh, *you* decide,' he said. 'I shall like anything that you like.'

'A Girtin, for instance?'

He gave me a wan smile.

When the menu had been ordered, with very little help on Gilbert's part, I returned to the charge.

'Oh yes,' I got him to admit 'I *could* have kept them—Aunt

Clare's treasures, I mean. But what good would they have done me? I work *against* something, not *for* something. I don't want the way made easy for me.'

'You mean you want to *keep* your sense of grievance, Gilbert? Your aunt put you over a barrel, as they say, when she tried to take it away. Either way, if you had kept her legacy yourself, or distributed it—or some of it—to your friends, as you so generously have—you would have felt at peace with the world. If,' I went on, 'I had ever been in a position to do anyone a good turn, to say nothing of doing several people a good turn—I should have lost my sense of grievance.'

'But you haven't one,' said Gilbert, almost as if he was pitying me.

'No, thanks to my temperament, I haven't. But my painting might be better if I had. I might even be angry, an angry middle-aged man. But if I had had a sort of universal aunt, who had enabled me to do a good turn to all my friends worth doing a good turn to—'

'Yes?' asked Gilbert.

'I suppose I should have lost my sense of grievance,' I concluded, lamely.

'And lost your talent with it?'

'How can I tell? Is grievance an essential ingredient of art?'

'With me it is,' said Gilbert.

Looking round at the other lunchers, intent on their food, with as much expression of distaste as his mild features were capable of, he said, 'You liked the little Girtin, didn't you?'

'Of course, Gilbert, I've told you so, again and again.'

'And Eileen and Adrian, they liked the Vuillard?'

'Oh yes, they adored it.' I didn't add, even to the point of selling it immediately.

'And the Dankervilles. Henry and Antonia, they liked the Munnings?'

Here I was on firmer ground. 'They couldn't have liked it more. Henry even said' (this I invented) 'that he would rather look at that horse, than ride himself, or hunt, or go to the Derby, or the Grand National, or wherever horsey-minded people go to.'

Gilbert heaved a deep sigh. 'Now you see what I mean.'

'Frankly, Gilbert, I don't.'

'Well,' said Gilbert, screwing up his eyes as though trying to envisage an imaginary scene—'supposing you painted pictures quite different from the kind of pictures you do paint—supposing a burglar or a hooligan or some enemy of society broke into your room, and turned your quiet interior topsy-turvy, everything knocked sideways or standing on its head, and broken as well, so that it was quite unrecognizable,—or supposing you went out into some peaceful *paysage* that you were wont to paint, so faithfully, and found that an earthquake or a tornado had struck it, so that every valley had been exalted and every mountain and hill laid low, all the trees bending and groaning, or flattened out with their branches clutching the ground and their roots sticking upwards into the sky so that the whole landscape didn't remind you of anything and made nonsense to you—would you be able to paint it?'

'Honestly, Gilbert, I don't think I could.'

'No, because your visual sense is trained to look at things in a certain way, which isn't necessarily the way they *really* are. Then just imagine how I feel when a soundless calm descends and everything that I've fought for in my music—the vision of the human condition that kept it going—suddenly isn't there? An empty battlefield, without opposing armies or a shot fired.'

I understood Gilbert's dilemma.

'Has the impact of your aunt's legacy changed your attitude to music?'

'Changed it? It has killed it stone dead.'

'But there must be something in you,' I argued, 'that prompted you to these generous acts. Otherwise why did you do them? You were under no obligation to, were you? Your aunt didn't make it a condition of her Will?'

I knew I had no right to ask their question, knew that it was in the worst of taste; but it had haunted me, as to some extent it had haunted all of us, even Eileen and Adrian, and the Dankervilles, who in the exhilaration of receiving it seemed to have taken Gilbert's *largesse* more or less for granted. If his aunt had enjoined him to part with some, if not all, of her treasures, it might well have given him a grievance against us, and against her—for grievances are usually more emotional than reasonable, and nothing makes so much bad blood as money.

When he didn't answer I repeated the question.

'*Did* your Aunt Clare want you to give away her beautiful things, Gilbert? And,' I added craftily, 'might she not be disappointed, and even hurt, supposing she was still with us, if she knew you had? She might have felt that you undervalued— not her generosity, but her affection for you.'

Gilbert sighed and his light-brown eyes roved round their sockets as though seeking an outlet.

'What did you say?'

'I asked if your aunt really *wanted* you to part with her . . . her belongings. I assume—we assume—that she left them to you unconditionally, as a mark of her affection and regard.'

'Do you mean,' said Gilbert, frowning, as far as his strangely unlined features allowed him to frown, 'that I ought not to have given you that little water-colour?'

He had me there. What if he should ask me to give it back to him?

'Oh no, Gilbert, a thousand times no. But she was a friend of mine, to some extent, whereas . . .'

'It's quite true,' said Gilbert, 'that some of the . . . the others, were only names to her. But there were two considerations which I think may have influenced her. One was that all this *money*'—he pronounced the word with distaste—'this Rheingold, coming from who knows where, and who knows how—ought to be made available where it would *tell*, in different people's lives I mean. She was a much more personal person and much more private-spirited, as opposed to public-spirited, than she allowed herself to seem.'

'And what was the second consideration, Gilbert?

'Why do you press me, Edward? Surely it's my concern.'

'But you said there were two,' I protested, 'and as an old friend of yours, and very much your debtor,—I feel I have a right to know why—'

'Why what?'

I couldn't bring myself to tell him but I think he knew what I meant when he answered, hastily.

'My aunt thought I was at odds with life, as perhaps she herself was, and that by giving me this . . . this dowry, she would help me to come to terms with it. I should be a victor, not a victim, do you see? But she didn't understand me. What I really relied on, as a composer, was my victimization. Yes, you may laugh, Edward, but it hasn't helped me to feel that you, and some other of my friends, are better off and possibly happier because of me, or what Aunt Clare has given me.'

'I am *much* happier,' I said, 'if that's any comfort to you. And so are the others. Don't you feel great gales of gratitude—the world's thanks—breathing down on you, blessing you, urging you to feel what a fine fellow you are?'

He made an impatient movement with his head, as if his collar chafed him.

'They breathe down my neck,' he said.

'Gilbert,' I insisted, 'why do you think your aunt left you those things—I know she was fond of you—instead of leaving them to this person, and that person, or to an institution?'

Gilbert hesitated.

'I suppose she wanted to make me happy.'

'But she hasn't?'

'Oh, Edward, I've explained it all to you. Don't let's go on chewing at it. She thought I should find happiness in other people's happiness—but it hasn't turned out that way. It isn't that I don't want other people to be happy,— I do, but if I have made them happy,—if I have made *you* happy—it somehow confuses me, because my talent—if you call it such—isn't based on happiness, in any form. Edward, I must go.'

'Oh no, don't go,' I said, seeking for some expedient to detain him.

46

'Isn't there anyone—'

'Anyone?'

'Anyone you *haven't* done a good turn to?'

'There is,' he said, rising. 'There are two, as a matter of fact, two who have so far escaped the curse of Aunt Clare's legacy. Two, just two, or one and a half. Don't ask me who they are.'

The commissionaire called me a taxi.

'Can I give you a lift?' I said.

'No thanks, dear Edward,' he replied. 'I go the other way from you.'

Chapter Six

So GILBERT hadn't given Myra a present. Why not, why not? Unusual, almost unheard of as it is to be annoyed with someone for not giving someone else a present, I was indignant with Gilbert on Myra's behalf. All along she had been his mainstay, the source of inspiration and reassurance that only a woman can be; and yet he had not made her the smallest material token of gratitude. Nor to Barbara. One and a half of his friends had received no bounty from Aunt Clare. Was Barbara the half? Barbara was useful to him, in her practical way, but far less important to him as an artist and a man, than Myra was.

When I thought of his ingratitude to Myra my blood boiled. How differently, in his place, I should have acted! I should have given Myra the chief of Aunt Clare's treasures, whatever it was, and been proud, yes, proud, to hear her say, 'Thank you.' Rotten fellow! But was there some bond between them, black-mail on his side, and on hers the fear of losing him, that excluded a gift? Must she remain his victim, the parasite on which he fed, so long as he gave her nothing?

It was like a kind of myth or fairy-tale, in which the heroine, the princess, is held captive by the gnome's refusal to give her a share in his ill-gotten gains. She would be free, I told myself, she would be free of him, if only he gave her something, however small, that discharged his debt to her. Then she would get her quittance; until then she would continue to be his slave—his slave of the lamp, for I knew he burnt the midnight oil.

But how to free her? I could not go up to Gilbert and say 'You must give Myra a present.' In some moods, the moods of his harshest musical compositions, he was quite capable of replying: 'Mind your own business' and of hitting me in the eye,

48

as indeed he would have every right to; and in any case, though he had not forbidden me the house, he had made it fairly clear that my presence was not welcome.

I should have to find an accomplice; but who was it to be? It must be someone, I felt, who had partaken of Gilbert's and his aunt's bounty: anyone outside that charmed circle would seem to be fishing—for themselves as well as for Myra. There were Henry and Antonia, Eileen and Adrian. A woman would be best; women are more diplomatic than men, and it must obviously be someone who knew Myra and was familiar with the whole set-up. Of the two, Antonia was the better bet; she was more intelligent and more perceptive than Eileen, who would be unable to resist dwelling on the money side of the transaction, rather than on its sentimental side; and this would not recommend itself to Gilbert, who whatever else he wanted to give, did not want to give money, certainly not to Myra, who had plenty of it. For the moment I forgot that Myra must not be a party to the secret: it would ruin the whole plan if she was.

But would Antonia fall in with the idea? She, like me, was under sentence of partial banishment, though no doubt, being a woman, she would find her way back to Gilbert's favour more easily than I should. She had her own theory about Gilbert's behaviour, a mistaken one, as I thought. She believed he was in flight from himself, and that was why he wanted to dispose of his aunt's possessions, if they were his to dispose of. She thought of him as desiring a state of utter spiritual nudity, like that of a Buddhist, in order that he might be the more free to pursue his art. But I was sure she was wrong; it was *us* he wanted to dispose of, not because we were an obstacle to his horrible music, but because without *us,* and his obligation to us, he wouldn't suffer from the irritation that his muse, and his music, needed. He wanted to write music, and he wanted peace of mind, but they could not be had together. That was his dilemma.

Each of us represented something, some human relationship that Gilbert didn't know how to deal with: by distributing his aunt's possessions, he was getting rid of us, not of them. We were the grains of grit that irritated the oyster into producing its ill-matched pearls, and deep in himself, he knew this and although he longed for peace of mind, as we all do,—and had paid us off with a Girtin, a Vuillard, a Munnings and so on—he knew that by doing so he was robbing himself of the prime source of his inspiration and that was why he hadn't given a present to some of his friends, notably not to Myra.

I tried to conjure up the big untidy room, with its piano and its harpsichord and its clavichord, in which he composed his horrible inventions. How many pictures, how many other miscellaneous *objets d'art* were stored there awaiting distribution? I should never know and perhaps Myra would never know.

The thing was to find someone who could persuade Gilbert that he ought to give Myra a share in his aunt's legacy. A share, *her* share: for everyone I spoke to thought that of all his friends she had the best claim. Aunt Clare, from her throne on high (it was impossible to think of her occupying a lesser position in Heaven than she had on Earth) must certainly be saying: 'Gilbert, you must give something to Myra. It is my *wish*.' Whether she had laid it on Gilbert as an obligation as well as a wish, we could not tell: but her wish it must have been. She had always liked Myra, probably of all Gilbert's friends Myra was the one she had liked the most. The Titian or whatever it was, (for none of us had been invited to inspect the remaining objects of Aunt Clare's bequest) should certainly go to Myra.

But how delicate, as well as how difficult, it was. Myra was well-off; she had a great many treasures of her own. She certainly had no Titians, or other objects in that category of value, but she had lots of lovely things, both in the house she deprecatingly referred to as her 'country cottage', and in her flat in London. Would she want to add to them? Would she want to feel 'obligated' as our American cousins say, either to Gilbert or to his *directrice*, Aunt Clare, (if she was his *directrice*) for adding to her heritage? I doubted it, and so did many others.

The accepted theory was, and it had strengthened since her death, that Aunt Clare had wanted Gilbert to marry Myra. Her own marriage had not been happy, her widowhood had been unhappier, but like many women she believed that an unhappy marriage was preferable to no marriage at all.

But had we any reason for thinking that Myra would fall in with this view? There was no evidence that Gilbert had ever proposed to her, or she to him. They were in their middle forties, and surely by now they knew their own minds. The fact that Gilbert had been a comparatively poor man (though always with expectations from his aunt), and Myra, if not a rich woman, quite comfortably off, made no difference. He was known as a composer, and his work was always a subject of controversy: he had something to offer to Myra, even if she had more to offer him. This had been the situation for many years: and was it likely that Myra would change her mind if Gilbert had bribed her with his reputed Titian (this picture had never been heard of until Aunt Clare died, and many doubted its existence).

Myra was a woman of proud and delicate feelings: supposing Gilbert had asked her to accept something from his aunt's bequest, would she have accepted it?

My thoughts ran on. In a situation of this sort, a situation involving the feelings, a man's sympathies are almost bound to go out to the woman. A man can, like the Lincolnshire poacher, jump out anywhere, whereas a woman can't, she has to bide her time and seek her opportunity, which often doesn't occur or used not to, and in any case she has more to lose, personally and socially, by taking the first step, or any step—than a man has. At least, this was once so. I could not imagine Myra wanting to marry Gilbert because he had given her—or his aunt had given her—an 'important' painting, any more than I could imagine that Gilbert would have given it her with matrimony in view.

*

Just as there exists the situation as it is,—the ordinary human situation—so there is always a corresponding but ideal situation to compare it with—the best thing that could happen. Aunt

Clare may have thought that the ideal solution would be for Gilbert and Myra to marry: I didn't. I thought that marriage, if successful, would be dangerous to Gilbert's gifts, which throve on personal maladjustment, and fatal to Myra's happiness, which depended on a delicate balance of relationships. His reason, I felt, for not giving her a present (which would have to be the best he had to give) was that by doing so he would lose her, and not only her, but the role of *agent-provocateur* that for some reason she, as we all to a lesser extent, played in his emotional, and creative life. His unconscious awareness of this made him hang back as a donor; and her consciousness of it made her hang back as a recipient: otherwise the presentation would long ago have taken place. I thought Gilbert was a dog-in-the-manger holding on to Myra simply because she, by the very qualities in her which he found the most discordant, inspired his muse. I couldn't believe that he was trying to keep her on tenterhooks, dangling in front of her some alluring and valuable carrot, to make her show her paces, and thereby encourage his. But if he didn't want her for herself but only as a vitamin and a pep-pill, there was someone who did.

*

It was then I thought of Barbara, Barbara my friend of many years, who was also Gilbert's friend and Myra's friend. I hadn't seen her for some time, I didn't even know whether Gilbert had 'bunched' her with a bouquet. That was the first thing to find out.

At once Aunt Clare, who was never far from my mind, prowling and prowling around like the hosts of Midian, invaded it again. I felt she must be appeased and placated, and if such an expression could be applied to so august a personage, she must be *pleased*, alive or dead. Barbara was an interior decorator; she had done up 'Poor Clare's' house in Kensington Square and she had given satisfaction. She had kept the large rooms rather empty, and the small rooms rather full, of pictures and other objects, I mean; it was one of her principles. Aunt Clare herself hadn't much idea of how to furnish a house, but she had the wherewithal, in every sense, and she left the arrangements to Barbara. Barbara came to think that Aunt Clare must be presented to her guests, her hangers-on, and to the world at large, against a rather neutral colour-scheme, however rich its adornments, so that when she rose to her feet, and took a few steps forwards to whoever it was, her surroundings should recede and she should precede. Her little laugh of welcome (I remembered it vividly) would then be most effective against a background of off-white, off-green or off-grey, if you see what I mean: she was old and rather wraithlike, and it wouldn't suit her to compete with any colour. A rather empty but expensive greenhouse, with a bust or two and plants pushed back to the glass walls—this was the effect that Barbara aimed at, and the elderly Undine would glide forwards in an atmosphere that wasn't exactly sub-aqueous, but that had an under-water feeling.

Barbara was, of course, in trade, which at one time might have counted against her socially: but Aunt Clare, who had once been poor herself, poor Clare!—before she had been wafted into the regions of the very rich, where social distinctions cease to have much weight, liked her all the same and did not dream of high-hatting her when she came in with her pencil and her drawing book, and made little sketches, with Aunt Clare, a vague silhouette, sitting or standing, against the tall windows which seemed to bring the outside world into the room.

Had she, through Gilbert, or had Gilbert, through her, left anything to Barbara? Gilbert had spoken of *two* people, or rather, one and a half, to whom he had made no present. Myra was the one; was Barbara the half? Barbara was formidably honest, in thought, word and deed; nothing would have persuaded her to sacrifice her integrity, even to Gilbert.

Chapter Seven

'YES,' Barbara told me as we lunched together, 'Gilbert did give me a keepsake, something that his Aunt Clare had left him. Sweet of him, wasn't it? And sweet of her too. Such lovely things she had—that Rembrandt etching of the Death of the Virgin—'

'I remember it,' I said. 'Has he given it to you?'

'So heavenly,' Barbara went on, 'so moving. Perhaps he will give it to Myra. She has never been married, and I have, once. I couldn't claim a title to virginity and all that pathos, that wonderful death-bed scene, with the Apostles and the doctors below, and above, all the host of Heaven looking down at me, eager to waft me to the skies! I wonder if Gilbert's Aunt Clare saw herself lying on that huge four-poster, with doctors and saints and angels all ministering to her! In a way she was rather a virgin herself, wasn't she?'

'She was married to Uncle Alfred,' I said.

'Yes, Edward, and I'm sure she was a good wife to him, if only a wife in name. I think he'd been through all that before he married her. She was his greatest ornament, lovely you know, with all that distinction of appearance, which he so sadly lacked.'

'But she needed something else,' I said.

'Perhaps, but for him she had what it takes—and he behaved like a gentleman to her, didn't he? He left her all those things,— I suppose he might have left them to other women.'

'No comment,' I said.

'Gilbert was her favourite, I suppose she felt he had more go and gusto than—than—. She liked those qualities, otherwise she wouldn't have married Alfred.'

'Have you seen Gilbert,' I asked her, 'lately?'

She stopped to think.

'Well no, since he brought me the tea-pot—in his own hands, mark you, so sweet of him—the tea-pot his aunt used for her early morning tea—a Crown Derby tea-pot—I haven't seen him. Nor have I seen anyone who *has* seen him, except *de passage*.'

'A teapot?' I said, surprised. 'That wasn't much of a present. Perhaps he has given The Death of the Virgin to Myra.'

There was a faint sound of jealousy in Barbara's voice as she said, 'I wouldn't know, I'm not in a virgin's secrets. Myra means a great, a great deal to him, much more than a Rembrandt etching, and still more than a teapot, however dear the teapot's associations may be.'

She stopped, and laughed.

'Do you think it's a kind of myth, something that Gilbert's afraid of, that if you give someone something, they will have to pay a forfeit? And that's why he hasn't given Myra anything, so far as we know? It might be, in a fairy-tale.'

'You won't be in much danger,' I said, 'from your teapot. I shall be in more, on account of my Girtin. But Myra will be in more danger still, seeing that she hasn't had *anything,* so far as we know.'

'Perhaps he's not afraid for her,' suggested Barbara, 'he's afraid for *himself.*'

'Afraid for himself? What *do* you mean? What *could* he give her, fairy-story-wise, that endangered him more than it endangered her?'

'It's not for me to say,' said Barbara, putting on the cloak of nothingness that she sometimes assumed. 'I have my teapot, you have your Girtin, Myra has—. Can't you draw your own conclusions?'

'Frankly, no,' I said.

There was a pause, and then Barbara asked:

'You haven't seen Gilbert lately?'

I shook my head.

'Nor have I. Have *you* not set eyes on him?'

'No, not properly. It's Myra he really cares for.'

'Perhaps we shan't see him again, not properly,' said Barbara, imitating the inflexion in my voice. 'Unless he thinks my efforts to interpret his musical notation worth a teapot.' She paused.

'But you, Edward, you must put all this away from you.' 'London starves the visual sense—forgive me,—my mind, if I have any, went off at a tangent. Now this restaurant, where we are sitting after the wonderful meal you've given me, is quite pretty, with all these murals of exotic scenes, chimpanzees and gorillas and kangaroos and ostriches and tigers, all disporting themselves under these fabulous banyan trees and palm trees and casuarina trees, but they don't make up for what one misses with the naked eye, so to speak.'

'You don't like London vistas?' I asked.

'I do, in a way,—your flat has a charming view over de Clore Gardens, but even there you have to apply your imagination so much to what you see, it's rather as though a visitor in modern Rome should try to see the Eternal City through the eyes of Piranesi. The view doesn't give you as much as you, to get something worth looking at, have to give *it*. Do I make myself plain?'

'Yes, Barbara.'

'Good. And in London one takes what one sees (if one sees anything in the intervals of jumping up on to a bus, or plunging down into the Tube)—you, of course, always use taxis, I shouldn't know so well what the view from a taxi is.'

'Very restricted,' I said, 'and one keeps wondering if the driver is going the right way. Do you think that Poor Clare ever travelled by bus or tube, or even by taxi?'

'Yes, in her youth,' said Barbara, 'in her youth I expect she had to walk. Walking sharpens the visual sense, not only to avoid getting run over, but to see—well, what there *is* to see. You approach it gradually, and gradually it sinks into you. Think of the experience of approaching de Clore Gardens on foot! I've done it often. First there is the long straight line—so impressive—of Bearsted Avenue, then the sudden, quick, dramatic turn into Cottesmore Close, then the back—doubles through the thug-haunted side streets, and then, the *revelation* of de Clore Gardens!'

I laughed, as Barbara meant me to.

'But of course,' she went on, 'during the long drawn out approach one has to see oneself—Barbara Newhouse, in my case—contributing vigorously to the view. It doesn't impose itself as it does in your charming, your delicious water-colours. You have, so to speak, to *invent* it, using the materials in sight, and quite often they're non-cöoperative, they assert their native ugliness against one's aesthetic sense, whereas when I go into a bare empty room, four walls, a floor, a ceiling, a door, a window, there is nothing to oppose my vision of what it should be, nothing to shut my eyes to, as there so often is, in London.'

'Was Aunt Clare easy to work for?' I asked.

'Oh yes, she was. She didn't make many concrete suggestions, but as I went with her from room to room, I got an idea, just from looking at her and talking to her, of what would really suit her. I was, and am, fond of strong colours,—you can't have too much red and gold and ultramarine for me. They would have set off, I thought, her shadowiness, but she didn't want that, she wanted to be a shadow among shadows, the ghost of her great possessions. I suppose she was seventy then, and her arthritis showed in every movement. She suffered, but the suffering gave her an extra dignity. It was like a suit of clothes that Nature had designed for her, and that didn't need the *imprimatur* of fashion, any more than pearls do.'

I told Barbara that I appreciated this picture of Aunt Clare. (I often forgot to say, 'Gilbert's aunt!') 'I agree that her wealth, or the legend of her wealth, made her half-mythical, but she had a hard-headed side.'

Barbara agreed.

'She was supposed to have said to a titled woman who was rude to her, "My name may not be as good as yours, but it's better at the bottom of a cheque."'

'She must have been very much provoked,' I said, 'to have allowed herself such an uncharacteristic witticism.'

'Perhaps the story is apocryphal. Certainly I don't remember her being rude to anyone,' said Barbara. 'She had no need to be. Of course she was always rather detached—and some people take that for rudeness.'

'How did she feel towards Myra?' I asked.

'Oh, Edward, you would know as well as I, or better. She liked Myra, as most of us do. They had something in common besides wealth, which is a great bond—she didn't feel that Myra wanted something from her, as rich people are so ready to feel about their friends.'

'You don't think that Aunt Clare wanted to give her—leave her—anything?'

'Leave her anything?'

'In her Will, I mean.'

Barbara thought this over.

'I shouldn't know. She left you something, and me something, and several other friends of ours—'

'No, Barbara, if you will excuse me, she didn't leave us *anything*. She left her money to Alfred's relations, who had the first call on it. But she left her *objets d'art* to Gilbert, as far as we know, not to us.'

'As far as we know?' asked Barbara. 'Don't *you* know, Edward?'

I answered with mounting irritation, 'No, I don't know. Gilbert, for whatever reasons, though I have my suspicions what they were, distributed her legacy among his friends. But he hasn't given anything to Myra, one of his closest friends, and one of his aunt's closest friends,—or if he has, we haven't been told.'

'And what conclusion do you draw from that?' asked Barbara.

'None, but I'm puzzled.'

'She may have thought that Myra had plenty of things already,' Barbara said.

'Yes, but that has never prevented rich people from endowing each other. Money goes to money. She could have left Myra some quite worthless memento with *Forget Me Not* on it, a keepsake. Victorians were fond of exchanging keepsakes. They felt that a keepsake was a sort of *aide-mémoire* to affection—'

'Yes, but you forget that she left these things to Gilbert. He has had the disposal of them.'

'I don't forget,' I said, 'and I feel that Myra may feel hurt at being overlooked.'

'Have you any reason for thinking that?' Barbara shot at me.

'No, but doesn't it stand to reason? We have all of us been enriched by, or through, Aunt Clare, but Myra hasn't. She may well ask herself why.'

'Oh, Edward, I don't think she would. She is the least mercenary, or envious, or jealous of women. Has she said anything to make you think?—'

'She greatly admired my Girtin.'

'Well, anyone would.'

'And she did say, rather wistfully, "What pretty things Clare had." I do feel that one of us should drop a hint to Gilbert—'

'Why not you, dear Edward?'

'No, I couldn't. You see, he has rather fought shy of me since he gave me the picture, as if to say, "One Girtin is enough. It discharges my responsibility to Edward." '

'But I haven't seen him lately, either. A Crown Derby teapot may not be so valuable as a Girtin water-colour—'

'Don't let's go into that, Barbara,' I said firmly. 'I'm a man, and you are a woman. I think it's a woman's job—women's work is never done—how ambiguous that is, I mean that after all their efforts, women have something left to do, whereas men just shut the office door with a clang, and that's that. *Basta, finito!* It's you, Barbara who should say in Gilbert's private ear, "I think, Gilbert, that Myra doesn't quite understand why"—but you would know how to put it much better than I can.'

'You have no office-door,' said Barbara. 'You're at liberty to work as long hours as you please. And I really don't want to remind him of his duty, or whatever you think it is, to Myra. I should feel such a fool, and interfering as well. There are things— quite harmless in themselves,—that people simply *don't do,* such as asking for a present back. And another thing they don't do is to ask a friend to give another friend a present. Of course if there are exceptional circumstances, if the other friend is hard up, for instance, and the first friend didn't know about it (oh dear, I get so muddled with these friends), but you can't pretend that Myra is hard up. She's about as hard up as, well, as St. Paul's Cathedral is.'

I saw an opportunity here.

'I daresay it is as hard up, as many cathedrals are. You've hit on an unfortunate example, Barbara. Myra may not be a cathedral, but she deserves maintaining as much as any cathedral, more for instance than Rochester, which is not one of my favourites.'

'I've never seen Rochester,' said Barbara petulantly, 'though I'm sure you're right about it. I can't think of a single feature it has that other cathedrals don't have. A nave, transepts, a choir, I'm not sure if it has a West Front—'

'Nor am I,' I said, 'but if it had, we should know. Myra has no West Front—'

'Oh, but you're wrong,' interrupted Barbara, 'a West Front is just what she *has*. She has no East End, to speak of, I won't dwell on that—but her West Front is magnificent, you could almost compare it to Peterborough.'

'Good heavens!' I exclaimed, thinking of the spires and turrets and gables over the three great arches. 'But I see you don't really like Myra. You're just being malicious about her.'

'I'm fond of her, I am,' protested Barbara.

'You aren't. Or you would ask Gilbert to give her the Leonardo he has stowed away in his airing cupboard.'

'But how can I ask him,' protested Barbara, 'if he doesn't want to see me? And I'm sure there's no Leonardo.'

'You could ask him to lunch.'

'So could you,' retorted Barbara in her *gamine* manner.

'I could, but it wouldn't be the same, and I doubt if he'd come. A woman is more persuasive with a man than a man is.'

'What an extraordinary remark, and how oddly you phrase it.'

'Do ask him, Barbara,' I begged. 'I feel as if the whole of his aunt's intention in leaving him the pictures will be frustrated if he doesn't give something to Myra. She will turn in her grave—'

'But she was cremated!'

'That's just a quibble,' I said, as severely as I could. 'But may I make this last appeal, dearest Barbara. Please, *please*, ask him.'

Barbara reached about for her bag, which, as so often happens, was much closer to her chair than she thought it was. Having retrieved it, she rose.

'I'm so sorry, Edward,' she said, in a quite different tone. 'But I really can't ask Gilbert to do what—what you want me to ask him to do!' She looked down at the floor, and then up at the ceiling. 'It would be too embarrassing, I am sure that when you think it over you will agree with me.'

'Very well,' I said, opening the door for her, 'in that case, I must take the law into my own hands.'

'What law?' asked Barbara, on her way to the lift. I didn't answer, but I had already made my plan.

Chapter Eight

BUT I didn't divulge my plan at once, even to myself. I kept chewing on it, and wondering how it would turn out, without quite knowing what it was. It kept appearing before me, as sometimes at bedtime a shape appears before one's closed eyes, and won't be exorcized,—it is seldom the augury of a peaceful night. A peaceful night should impose its own darkness behind one's eyelids.

The plan itself turned out to be quite simple, as many plans are. It was the details which should put the plan into execution, that needed working out. You may plan to murder someone— more and more people do. To murder Gilbert, perhaps?

Perish the thought. What could have put such a notion into my head?

No, but Gilbert must somehow be eliminated from Myra's life—he must leave her free, free for me, Edward. And the simplest way of making him do this—relinquish her—was by persuading him to give Myra something—something, no matter what.

It must be more than the token-present, the Crown Derby teapot, with which he had fobbed off Barbara—a present needing a thank-you letter, but no more: a pretty acknowledgement of their mutual indebtedness that left their original relationship in *status quo*, Gilbert the master, Barbara the slave. He would still be the dictator, in both senses of the word, and she the scribe.

But if it was a more considerable gift, a gift that couldn't be disregarded because, in vulgar parlance, it stank of money, then Myra would be liberated from her thraldom to Gilbert, and he from his obligation (or whatever it was) that bound him to her.

But clearly for various reasons,—reasons of affection, psychological reasons, reasons of self-interest,—he didn't mean to give her anything—not even a teapot. He meant to keep her to himself, and didn't dare to risk the passport to freedom which a gift implies. 'You have accepted this from me—now we are quits.'

I couldn't go to Gilbert, estranged as we appeared to be, and say, "You must really give Myra something. She will be terribly hurt if you don't. All the public opinion of our little group will be *outraged* unless you give her something." But I *could* say to her, "Gilbert has asked me to give you the Girtin water-colour of the Pantheon in Paris which he has temporarily—just temporarily —lodged with me. I like it very much, and I am flattered at being asked to give it house-room; but to tell you the truth" (and this was true enough) "it doesn't fit in with my other pictures. It belongs (how shall I say it without seeming too pompous?) to a higher category of art. So the sooner you can come here and collect it, dear Myra, the better, unless you would rather I brought it to you? I always need an excuse for seeing you, and a reason for doing Gilbert a good turn. He is so devoted to you, the dear fellow, and I wonder why he made me an intermediary for the Girtin, which will look so much more at home among your beautiful things than it does here with my junk?"'

Gilbert, when the Girtin water-colour arrived at Myra's flat, couldn't deny my story: he couldn't say to her, to her above all people, 'I never meant to give this picture to you, and I don't want you to have it.' All he could say (for he was quite civilized in social relationships though not in music) would be, 'How kind of Edward to have kept the picture for you, dear, dearest Myra. I felt he would enjoy looking at it for a little while, for besides being an ideal storehouse for pictures, he is a painter in his own right, isn't he? But for him it was just a *loan*, such as many painters make to art-galleries (and what a lot of pictures Edward has! Almost *too* many, I would think), and I am more than glad to know that it has passed its uneasy moment of transition, and found its real home, the home I always destined it for, with *you*, darling Myra.'

But might Gilbert feel he ought to give me something in place of the Girtin? I should not ask him, of course, but he might feel he owed it me. If he didn't, his expressed wish, (expressed by *me* that is) that I should give my picture to Myra would put him in rather a bad light, unless he promised to compensate me for my loss. She could say to Gilbert, 'Possibly you were thinking of giving Edward some little thing in exchange?'—she knew him quite well enough to say that, indeed she knew him very well, too well, in my opinion.

Then I should have gained twice over: I should have recovered Gilbert's friendship, which I valued, for he could still feel that he had paid me off (if that was what he wanted to feel),—since it was no business of his that I had given his picture to Myra. And, secondly, he would have to accept the fact that Myra had been paid off, although vicariously; she could no longer be a charge on his conscience, as I suspected she was, his secret source of inspiration,—if I was right in believing that his creative faculty came of a sort of love-hatred relationship between him and his friends. The thought of them made him furious. Bang! Crash! the room or the concert-hall shuddered. Paid off by a picture, they couldn't molest him, but they could minister to his desire for peace which (I guessed) had always been at odds with his creative urge. He had no reason to think he had been a failure: his music had been acclaimed by the critics, and even patronized by the public; but pushing up the fifties, one isn't so intent on quarrelling for the sake of producing a work of art. 'Peace, peace, Orestes-like I breath this prayer,' as Longfellow wrote. And Gilbert, who had been driven into music by the Furies (by us, or his innate disapproval of us), was longing for the time when he had no friends to irritate and madden him, and could sit in his studio as a deaf person might, surrounded by instruments of music but with no desire whatever to make them heard, still less to perform on them himself.

'Peace, perfect peace, with loved ones far away,'—that was Gilbert's aim, the aim to which a part of him was striving; but another part, the Puritan part (for he had been brought up a

64

Nonconformist) said 'No, go labour on, spend and be spent,' and that was why he still retained the 'services' of Myra. As long as she was the grain of grit inside his shell, he might still produce a pearl.

But I liked her too much to relish this ignominious role for her. With me she would be the pearl ready-born, the pearl of great price. She would be that to me, for my gift, such as it was, consisted in reconciliation, harmony, *unity* with what I saw and felt and tried to put down in rather weak colours.

An American writer of the last century said, 'Before you become a rogue, you should decide if you have better qualifications to be a fool.'

Was I, Perseus, a fool to try to rescue Andromeda from her rock? I didn't think so, but in order to get, as more and more people do nowadays, an intimate satisfaction from a doughty but dubious deed, I had to consider objectively the ways and means.

Besides my preoccupation with Myra, and my resolve to rescue her from her demon-lover, I had my own career to consider, my belated career as a painter, if I still had one. That London starves the visual sense is only too true. What is known is taken for granted, it is predigested, a safe diet for a tired stomach, not a nourishing or exciting one, whereas what is springing up, up, up to take its place—the sky's the limit—*that*, my feeble powers of versatility and adaptability could never assimilate. I could not acclimatize myself to it; I must go elsewhere; and where better than to Italy, where so many foreign painters have found what they were looking for. Not Girtin, alas; he got no further than Paris. Paris was not paradise to me but Italy was, and I lingered there even when I realized that it was not a paradise for a water-colour painter of my type. Turner had been able to capture the dynamic quality of the landscape, and even add his own imagination to it; Alexander Cozens had made Rome and the country round it, the dark lake of Nemi enfolded by its hills, fascinating to an English eye; Sargent had painted water-colours of Venice that are more *like* Venice (if likeness is a recommendation nowadays) than the pictures of Guardi or Canaletto—they had the watery gleam and the hint of bad weather which the Italians (perhaps because they were used to it) hadn't noticed. Moreover, the Italians didn't favour water-colours; theirs was a major art, suited to oils and tempera and the other media they used for presenting what they looked at in the grand manner. Compared to theirs, water-colour was a miniaturist art, a matter of searching out and emphasizing fine shades of meaning which would have made their mark under a chilly, lightless Northern sky, but which would have escaped notice under the bright sunshine of Italy. And indeed, in spite of all the illustrious exceptions (to which the visiting Velasquez himself provided two), landscape for its own sake was not an art much favoured in Italy. The Italians were a passionate race, intensely human as well as humanistic, and though art of all sorts came natural to them, as natural as the air they breathed, and the sunshine that soaked into them, they could not so easily appreciate an art—the water-colourist's art,—which depended on trying to make a lot out of a little.

But inspiration (if I may use such a word) doesn't depend so much on forms of art, as on the material, the subject-matter of art, which is to be found more abundantly, and in stronger measure, in Italy than anywhere else. In Italy an artist, practising whatever art, is *someone*: in many countries (let us not say which) he is *no one*,—and that is why I decided to refresh my art, and if possible give it a new look by going to Italy. Assisi, I thought, shall be my headquarters—Assisi, as Nathaniel Hawthorne charmingly said, looked at night like a rosary flung against a hillside. I had known it a little, before the days of motor-traffic; now I should know it better. I could hardly wait to go.

If only Myra could go with me! But no, she was enslaved to Gilbert, not by his love or his affection for her, but by his need of her, which, if my interpretation was correct, was his muse's need, not his. His muse needed her, or his ambivalent relationship with her, to provide those strident and piercing yells which were a feature of his music, music that, in my opinion, had little to do with the Muse.

66

Why, I asked myself for the hundredth time, should Myra be sacrificed to the requirements of Gilbert's art, when she could so easily have lived a happy and peaceful life, devoid of dissonances with anyone, above all with me?

So it was that I went ahead, trying to foresee, and forestall, any mishap. Aunt Clare might have said, 'Whatever you do with the things I am going to leave you, Gilbert, and whatever use you put them to, please don't give anything to Myra Henning. I don't care for her, and would much rather that nothing of mine should ever belong to her.' That would be a facer; but I had two reasons for disregarding it. First, that Aunt Clare was known to be fond of Myra; and secondly that I did not mean to tell Gilbert of my intention; so if Aunt Clare did intervene, it would have to be by supernatural means, a message from the grave. All sorts of minor accidents might happen: the picture might be damaged in transit from my flat to Myra's; this danger would to some extent be overcome if I insured it heavily, and procured another Girtin with the insurance money. And if it was left outside the door of my flat with no one to receive it, and got stolen, the insurance would cover that, too.

There were other snags. Myra might misunderstand my motives or understand them all too well; she might say to herself, 'Edward isn't well off; how can he afford to part with this picture? There must be "something behind it."'

All these objections, and many more, I disposed of. It is such a simple operation to give someone something—it is the oldest interchange in the world, older than any business deal, for did not Eve give Adam the apple?—and as for social and personal embarrassments, they could all be covered by the proverb, 'You mustn't look a gift-horse in the mouth.'

*

All the same I wasn't happy about my intentions, and my thoughts shied away from them. I felt I was doing what I knew to be wrong. Perhaps Heaven thought so too, for my efforts to see Myra before I went abroad were frustrated: her dates would not fall in with mine nor mine with hers. Face to face, or better, hand in hand, we could have made a job of it. We shouldn't have had to analyse it, or refrain from analysing it: the destination of the Girtin and its meaning to us could have been decided with a look. Let sleeping dogs lie. Discussion brings into the open latent animosities which, if left alone, would have died a natural death.

Chapter Nine

BEFORE I left for Italy, I saw Barbara again, and we went over the old ground, Aunt Clare's bequests, as distributed by Gilbert, —the Girtin to me, the teapot to her, and to Myra, nothing.

'He wasn't very generous to you,' I said.

'To me? How can you say so? That ravishing teapot! Gilbert is the soul of generosity! Now if it had been Myra—'

'If it had been Myra?' I reminded her.

'Oh well, perhaps he would have given her something more . . . more substantial. Perhaps he has, perhaps he will, we don't know. I don't like thinking of human relationships in terms of a *quid pro quo*, do you?'

'Sometimes one has to,' I said.

'Yes,' replied Barbara, 'but it's ignominious. I don't want any reward for the little I do for Gilbert. Nor, I'm sure would Myra. Now you're off to Assisi—a place which *purges* one of the baser passions.'

'Let's hope it will,' I said, 'let's hope it will.'

Barbara suddenly turned away from me and said:

'How I should adore to go there! But I never shall, I never shall.'

'Not even if Gilbert was there to dictate his music to you?' I asked teasingly.

*

So I went to Assisi no forrarder than I had been, though no less determined that Myra should have the Girtin. Getting Gilbert behind me (or wherever Satan ought to be) forgetting him (as far as I could), simplifying the position to nothing more complicated than the bare fact of present-giving, made me happy: I looked forward to the moment when the picture should cease to be mine and become hers. I knew how much she liked it, for she had told me, and I longed for her to have it,—irrespective of any side-effects it might have on our relationship.

I found a comfortable hotel on one of the lowest zigzags of the town, with a heavenly view southwards over the plain of Perugia, and only a few hundred yards from the church of St. Francis. I had seen it before, but could not wait to see it again. The next morning I started off.

I was still beset by the demands of the visual sense, but I do not mean to describe, even if I could, my sensations as I climbed the white, dusty road, trodden by so many pilgrims to the church. Italian churches are not my favourite churches, whether Roman-esque, or Gothic, or Baroque. I feel that Italy, which has un-disputed sovereignty in so many arts, must give place to France and England in this one. Their churches seem to lack the sense of design and the sense of mystery, that northern churches have. And, too, they are less ecclesiastical and less religious, perhaps because there is less contrast between them and their surround-ings. They seem part of the street which so often they rise up out of: they are familiar, homely, almost domestic, part of the national heritage of living and thinking, not detached from it and above it, and belonging to another world, like our northern cathedrals.

But the church of St. Francis has its own personality and its own message, not only for the faithful. It enshrines his body, the body of one of the greatest well doers and well-wishers to humanity who has ever lived; and anyone who does not realize this, I reminded myself as I trudged upwards, past the arcades with the picture post-cards, under the glaring sun, must be unconscious of all that is most valuable in human nature. Was I unconscious of it? I asked myself.

As all visitors to Assisi know the church of St. Francis has a peculiarity shared by some other churches, by San Clements in Rome, by our own St. Paul's, for instance—it is two churches in one, or rather two churches one above the other; not a church with a crypt, which is usual enough, but an Upper Church and a Lower Church, each with its separate being, that contrasts violently and dramatically with the other. The Upper Church all sunlight, the Lower Church all shade, except for the Chapel behind the High Altar where there is light enough to see the pictures by.

To the Lower Church I bent my way. When I went in I could at first see nothing, so deep was the darkness after the blinding sunshine outside, then I began to discern the pictures which cover every inch of the ceiling. I asked myself, as I had asked myself twenty years before, how the artists were able to see what they were doing: did they work by candlelight, or lamplight, or by some inner light, which could take on physical properties and direct their brush-strokes? Was their eyesight better than ours? Or was the Italian genius, so intent on pictorial expression that it accepted physical handicaps not so much as a challenge as a condition of the painter's calling?

I moved on in the gloom, past the High Altar into the comparative brightness of the presbytery, and there on my right was what I was looking for, Simone Martini's gallery of portraits, a dozen or so of them, with St. Francis towards the left and St. Clare more or less in the middle. Pale and indistinct as it was, I remembered that reserved aristocratic haughty face, with its long eyelids and withdrawn look. It is the only portrait of her, as far as I know, in existence, and may have been as little like her as the portrait of St. Francis with his almost Chinese cast of features, is like the rough, vigorous little figure in the neighbouring picture by Cimabue.

Of the two it was Santa Chiara who interested me the more, for I thought I could trace a likeness between her and Gilbert's aunt. True, his aunt was not aristocratic but her wealth had lent her the same dedicated look of power and purpose and authority —the same severity too, though St. Clare had been severe and Aunt Clare to the best of my knowledge, except in social relationships, and charity, and will-making—quite a long list of exceptions!—was not. Will! There was plenty of will in both of them,

71

and in both senses of the word, for St. Clare must have had plenty of money to found her Order with, before she bestowed it on her votaries and, as they did, took the vow of poverty.

I sought a message from her portrait, painted with no intention to enhance its beauty or hers; and I thought I saw a look of disapproval and reproach, as though she knew what I was up to, and didn't like it. It may have been my sense of guilt in the presence of her holiness and sanctity; but it seemed more personal than that, as if she was warning me against something. Against what? Surely not against giving Gilbert's present—the present Aunt Clare had given to him and through him to me,—to Myra who would appreciate it so much—so much, indeed, that Gilbert would have no more claims on her? St. Clare must have given many presents in her day—her day of 700 years ago,—and were they not partly meant to relieve her of responsibility—of her debt to the Church, and to humanity, and to God for whose sake and for whose advantage she had deprived herself of her worldly goods?

So I reasoned, though I knew my reasoning was faulty, for St. Clare would only have desired spiritual gain—if indeed she would have desired that—for her benefactions, whereas I had a less admirable motive. But she could not have denied that a gift is a gift, and all the more meritorious when it is dear to its possessor, as the Girtin certainly was dear to me, and not only in monetary value, for I should miss it when it passed into Myra's keeping. Yes, its loss would give me a pang, even if the reward for parting with it was Myra herself.

I turned away from the presbytery with all its treasures of primitive art, and almost tiptoed up the narrow, dangerous staircase, worn by how many footsteps of the devout, as well as by sightseers and trippers. Trip was the word, for many must have taken a toss on their way. *There,* in the Upper Church, all was light and height and space and simplicity and gladness. Whether the tall pictures that lined the walls were by Giotto or by his 'school' I could not tell. Several guides, in several languages, were explaining them to hordes of tourists; this double frieze of highly dramatized sacred scenes was what the majority of visitors to Assisi wanted most to see. I gazed at them, of course, and marvelled at them, but my mind was still with Santa Chiara in the sombre caverns of the Lower Church. Before I left I went down by the balcony that overlooks the cloisters—grey stone and terracotta brick—and stood again before the picture of St. Clare whom I had begun to identify with Gilbert's aunt, but her look was still reproachful,—or reproving, perhaps I should say.

The public rooms of the hotel were intended for drink and gossip and flirtation rather than for writing: gone was the sober decoration I remembered; it had been replaced on the walls by seaside scenes strangely out of place and out of character in Assisi: everybody seemed to be on pleasure bent and celebrating a carefree holiday mood in semi-nudity under awnings and umbrellas and palm-trees, exchanging looks of love, or too sleepy, whether from idleness or satiety, even to do that. I wondered what St. Francis would have thought of them, I knew what St. Clare would. At last in despair of finding a table or even a corner to myself I retired to my bedroom and wrote, as I believe was the practice of Christina Rossetti, on a spare space on the dressing-table.

Dearest Myra,

I am so glad to be again in this holy little town, though not so holy or so little as I remembered it. But perhaps if I can summon the energy, to climb to where the Rocca frowns above, I shall have a different impression. At any rate there are now—an innovation since my time—plenty of taxis to take me. The hill looks much longer and steeper than it used to!

But I have paid my respects to St. Francis and St. Clare— to her picture in the Lower Church, I mean, not to the fane dedicated to her—*questo sarà per un altra volta* (I am trying to brush up my Italian). Her portrait reminded me in more ways than one of Gilbert's aunt, poor Clare as we used to call her. She doesn't look very benevolent, but neither did Aunt Clare, though actually she was—as you know better than I—being a closer friend of Gilbert's, and of hers too, I believe.

And this reminds me of another thing. Gilbert, as you know, inherited quite a number of her possessions—her very considerable possessions—which he proceeded, most generously, to share out with his friends. I was one of the lucky ones, as I expect you were too, though it would be impertinent to ask. Gilbert hasn't told me—why should he?—he was always rather reserved in some ways. But I have got it into my head that he once told me that you had an affection for Girtin's water-colour of the Pantheon in Paris, painted from the left bank of the Seine. It is a long, narrow picture in discreet shades of grey and green and pink. There are buildings in the foreground, some rather sombre, reflected in a solid manner, more simplified and more solid than the buildings themselves, in the river, which is as calm and smooth as a lake. Perhaps there were no steamers in his day, like *La Belle Jardinière*, which used to cause such a commotion in mine not only in the river but in the air, with piercing hoots and screeches, so that the reduplication (allowing for the differences which the artist's genius thought it necessary to make) is almost perfect.

I love the picture, and should love it still more if I thought it belonged to *you*, and I would have said something to Gilbert about this except that I haven't seen him, or only to exchange a word with and to thank—ever since he gave me the picture. As I said, I don't know what he has given you: he may have given you one of his Aunt's fabulous treasures—the Leonardo drawing or the Titian that she is said to have kept in the bathroom—on the grounds that no burglar would ever search a bathroom. Whether he has or has not is no business of mine, but in any case my great wish, dear Myra, is that you should have my Girtin: I shall enjoy it through your eyes more than I enjoy it through my own (which haven't been too good lately, though I hope that the bright sunshine here will give them a new lease of life).

Forgive this long preamble—but what I wanted to say was,

Will you accept the picture as a token of our long friendship? And would you explain to Gilbert (being out here I can't, very well), that I wanted you to have the picture, both as a gift from him and a gift from me? I'm almost sure he wants you to have it, and it would be easier for you to tell him than for me, in case he was surprised that I wanted to part with his gift—but he wouldn't be, I'm sure, he is much too generous-minded—and in his secret heart he will be delighted that the picture is where he always wanted it to be, in your house, looking at you. If as I suspect, he has already given you something else, never mind! The Girtin will be my gift, as well as his.

So I am writing to my factotum to ask him to take it to Hans Place—only I *should* be grateful if you explained to Gilbert that he has now made his present give happiness to *two* people. It will be easier for you because, as I said, you see him oftener than I do, and besides I am abroad. And this reminds me of something else. Would you feel inclined to pay Assisi a visit? I am here till the end of June, painting, I hope, most of the time, but what a joy it would be if in the intervals of work or, better still, while I *am* working you could add your sunlight to the scene and incidentally keep away those hordes of children who infest anyone in this country who is painting in the open air.

With so many hopes that this will come about, dear Myra, and with all my love,

Edward.

P.S. I said that the Girtin was a gift, but I have strong reasons for thinking it was a loan. Something Gilbert said to me (I can't confirm it, he is so elusive and evasive) convinced me that he really wanted *you* to have it, and only *lent* it to me as a temporary ornament to my 'collection'. Don't remind him of this—he is so odd and touchy nowadays—but I can assure you it is so. *You* were to be its ultimate destination, I, only its half-way house!

Chapter Ten

LUNCH was at hand. I ate out-of-doors on the terrace, looking down on the sunlit plain, with the great church of Santa Maria degli Angeli in the near distance. Could I paint the scene? I didn't think so, it was too broad and spacious for my rather minuscular treatment. And I was tired, tired by the journey; tired by my visit to the church of St. Francis, with its emotional undertones and overtones; tired by my letter to Myra, which seemed to have taken out of me something that I needed for climbing hills. Perhaps I had climbed a hill? I felt the sense of achievement that climbing gives. After a nap I did climb to the post office, at the end of the piazza, and put my letter in the letter-box. Nowadays the Italian post is so unreliable that I didn't expect an answer for many days. But I did send a telegram. 'Lovely here, dear Myra. Why not come out, and persuade Gilbert to come too? Letter in the post, With all my love—' I was going to sign it with my name, but I knew she would know who had sent it.

I didn't know what I expected to happen, and my mind was all the freer to find a stance for a picture. What better than the piazza of Santa Chiara, busy though it was? The flying-buttresses had always fascinated me—there are so few in Italy. Perhaps I could give an impression of their lightness and their strength. The wings of angels, or of devils?

Having sent the telegram I felt ashamed of myself, and couldn't understand why I had done it. Myra would be bewildered by it, for it would arrive long before my letter. If she interpreted it as an urgent need on my part to keep in touch with her she wouldn't be far wrong, but she would certainly be surprised. We had been good friends, even great friends, for many years, and she was far too sensitive and intelligent not to notice the change from the *status quo*.

Meanwhile Assisi was not starving the visual sense. I could feel my outlook changing with every step I took. Italy demands to be seen; the light, for one thing, accentuates visibility, and whereas in England you have to look for what you want to find, in Italy it is the other way round—a question of rejection rather than selection. Everything clamours to be seen, almost literally clamours, for the unrestrained noise seems to enhance the visibility. All the manifestations of life are like the landscape and the buildings, geared to a higher power than they are with us, and a painter must accept the challenge. A muted, low-toned picture of Santa Chiara, leaving out the glare, and the universal almost visible buzz and hum would give a false impression—it would be like attending a royal ceremony dressed in ordinary day clothes. The piazza on which Santa Chiara looks out is one of the noisiest, busiest places in Assisi. It throbs and vibrates with self-assertion, with the drama and rhetoric of the Italian temperament. I knew I must adjust mine to it, but I wondered if I could. It was so long since I had tried to paint out of doors, with a mob of children watching, and sometimes getting between me and my subject.

These unusual conditions stimulated me and sharpened my visual sense quite remarkably, and I began to allow myself a more declamatory style than the restrained, hush-hush approach I used in England, where I painted from inside outwards, making what I looked at reflect my moods, which didn't change very much, instead of letting what I saw determine them. Under this influence, you might say, leading from the solid, earth-bound pavement of the piazza to the heaven-pointing roof of Santa Chiara's shrine, I started to paint.

A day later I received a telegram: 'Making plans for Assisi but await your letter, MYRA.'

What a weight off my mind to know that she, more practical than I, had straightened out my clumsy muddle, and wouldn't come until she had given Gilbert my message. The barrier of self-hood which often gets in the way of creative work thus took another knock: Fate would accomplish what I had put in train. I only had to wait for its next move, and the tingling of anticipation bore my spirit upwards.

The day which brought Myra's second telegram announcing her arrival for tomorrow, also brought a letter from Gilbert.

'Myra has told me of your kind offer,' he wrote, 'to make over to her the little Girtin that Aunt Clare and I had meant for you. She said you thought I wanted her to have it, and that I had told you so. I don't remember doing that, dear Edward, your memory must be better than mine. I had always wanted to give Myra something belonging to Aunt Clare—but she is a difficult person to choose for, isn't she?—though not difficult to choose. The Girtin seemed just right for you, but somehow not for her: for her I wanted something more, more—what shall I say without the false impeachment that one of you has what the other lacks,—more impressionistic. Not necessarily newer or older. I had one or two things in mind, for Aunt Clare was nothing if not generous, but I couldn't decide between them, and when Myra told me about your Girtin, it put me in a quandary, for how could I say to her, 'No, don't take it. I want to give you something else?' So I made a rather non-committal answer which she could interpret how she liked—and honestly I don't know how she did interpret it, for she said no more, just looked out of the window as she sometimes does, hoping for inspiration.

Later she told me she might be joining you in Assisi, staying at the same hotel; in fact, that's how I came to know your address. Probably she will talk to you, about the picture, but perhaps she won't—or if you bring the subject up, she may just look out of the window! I have a sort of feeling that she may not want to join the crowd of Aunt Clare's beneficiaries, she may not want to receive a present at second hand, so to speak—and I myself don't much want her to! She has a special place in my life—she is a sort of Egeria, an inspiration, it's for her I write my music—it's a kind of offering, I compose with the thought of her in my mind, as I do, or did, for all my friends. Gratitude is a most precious and humanizing agency, don't you agree? Only one has to be rather cautious with it, and not treat it as an obligation to be shuffled off. Most men want to be emotionally independent, with women it's the reverse—but I don't want to be independent of Myra, that's why I have hesitated to give her—what I thought of giving her. I may still give it to her, but I would rather give it her direct if you see what I mean. I know you like her, perhaps you love her too. We mustn't get in each other's way—nothing about let the best man win! Your knight's move has rather cramped my style—not that I blame you, nor do I want to tie Myra's hands in any way.

Perhaps I have said too much, perhaps not enough—but when Myra comes to Assisi you will be able to sort things out. Myra said you wanted me to join you in that delectable city— I only wish I could.

With my love,
Gilbert.

P.S.
    Say a prayer to Santa Chiara for me.

I pondered over Gilbert's letter. If it was meant to make me feel a cad it certainly succeeded, for it was full of implied reproach. Yet what right had he to reproach me? Myra would have married him if he had asked her; it was said that it was on his account that she remained single; he used her for his art, his art which needed emotional unfulfilment. His art throve on anger and how could he be angry if he was united to Myra? Married to her he would lose his sense of loss and grievance, the chip on his shoulder, which he could still keep if she was his mistress, as some said she was. He needed to be at odds with himself. By giving way to the generous streak in his nature by which so many of us, his friends, had profited, he had forfeited his inspiration, or some of it; if he surrendered to his love for Myra, even to the

79

extent of giving her a present, he might lose it, and that he dared not risk. In a way she was his whipping-boy; she fostered the sense of incompleteness which found an outlet in his ugly music. It didn't appeal to me but it did, no doubt, appeal to people who were at odds with themselves and with the world.

So I figured it out. But why should Myra be sacrificed to this dog-in-the-manger, when there was at least one who knew a better way than his to be happy?

Yes, but there was the practical, the material side. Myra was well off; but would she want to forgo the major bequest that Gilbert was rumoured to have in store for her? She too must have heard report of it and would she thank me for interfering? She was by way of being a collector, and she might well prefer some Old Master with a resounding name to the more dubious privilege of being Gilbert's Egeria and/or mistress, supposing she was either? By spiking Gilbert's guns I might have turned her away from me, not towards me. I relied on Gilbert's not telling her that I had lied about the Girtin, because to have done so would have put him in an invidious position; but being an intelligent woman she might have seen through my ruse, and despised me for it instead of loving me. It was commonly thought that men were put off by women's machinations to ensnare them, whereas women were the opposite: they liked a man all the better for any large or small deceptions he practised in pursuing them. But would they, if it meant forfeiting some concrete treasure they had set their hearts on? In some ways women were as mercenary as men; from the earliest times love had been their trade as well as their occupation: they valued its material rewards as much as, or even more than men did. And the fact that they were more purposeful, more long-sighted and capable of greater acts of self-sacrifice in the field of love than men were, often meant they had an ulterior motive to which love was only a stepping-stone.

How explain the fact that Gilbert and I had reached our middle forties without getting married? Partly, no doubt, because each of us was married to the Muse, that jealous mistress; but was there also an undeclared rivalry between us for Myra's hand, a rivalry of which she was aware but could not, or didn't want to, terminate,—preferring the insecure but influential position at the centre of a see-saw holding the balance between two suitors?

*

'Signore!' said a voice at my elbow. I looked up, too deep in my thoughts to realize that the white-coated functionary was addressing me.

'Signor Eduardo!' he went on more urgently, and smiling as if the news could only be good news. 'There is a lady just arrived who desires to speak to you.'

'Oh,' I said, getting up. 'What is her name?' But I knew.

'She did not tell me.'

'Where is she?'

'In the Sunshine Bar, signore.' I followed him, with mixed feelings, into the Sunshine Bar.

She was sitting with her back to me.

'Myra!' I exclaimed, putting into my voice the warmth of welcome I hoped to hear in hers.

She must have been in the hotel some time before acquainting me with her arrival, for the apéritif on the table was nearly finished.

She got up slowly, and turned a rather grave face to me.

'Well,' she said, 'you see I'm here.'

Chapter Eleven

WE DINED together, and agreed to meet at twelve o'clock and motor to Perugia—not my favourite town, I much preferred Assisi, but Myra hadn't seen it. In the picture-gallery, which occupied us till lunchtime, we naturally talked of pictures; *the* picture wasn't mentioned between us, but it was so vivid to my mind that I sometimes thought I saw it on the wall, and Myra may have seen it too, for she was *distraite* and preoccupied, and made comments which hadn't much heart in them. I was glad when our tour of the tall gallery was over and set us free for a well-earned lunch. But the constraint continued, as I knew it must until we broached the subject of the picture. Time passed with leaden feet, as it always does when it is being cheated of its prey. I began to have a panic feeling, which I think Myra shared, that her visit would come to an end without either of us having said anything—anything to the purpose.

As the car zigzagged down into the sunlit plain I had never felt more out of tune with the traditional high spirits of Italy. Those high spirits are sometimes delusive, an example of the pathetic fallacy; they do not necessarily conform to the moods of the climate, whether for good or ill. But there is usually something definite and clear-cut about Italians; they proclaim their feelings by their looks. Certainly in most Italian pictures it isn't hard to tell whether the faces are bowed down by sorrow or alight with joy. They do, of course, prefigure intermediate states, wonder, doubt, astonishment and the like; but one feels that whatever they show is a reflexion of something that has happened to them, a reaction to an outside pressure. They are not creating their states of mind from within, as was the case with me, and I think with Myra. We didn't quite know what was the matter with us, or why we were turning a blind eye to Nature, which seemed to wish us to enjoy ourselves.

It has always been a failing of mine—Puritan, stoical—not to be able to respond to the more genial moods of the weather. In principle I approve of them, and loudly lament their absence, but in practice I can't live up to them, they raise existence to a higher power than I can attain to, and leave me sadly lacking in a sense of *joie-de-vivre*. *Joie-de-vivre*; does any Englishman, Puritan or not, really have it? If he ever had, it vanished with Merrie England, and I have often wondered whether there ever was a Merrie England, as there is, and perhaps always has been, a Merrie Italy. But I'm not sure. Lucretius wrote:

> 'Medio in fonte leporum
> Surgit amari aliquid,'

which means, I suppose, that there is always a drop of bitterness in the fountain of human happiness. 'To carry a knife now,' a policeman said to me, 'is like keeping up with the Joneses.'

Murder is the easiest crime to prove. If they think, I said to myself, eyeing the advancing horde of menacing motorists, that I am going to accommodate them by letting them run over me, they are very much mistaken.

*

Gilbert was always hurting himself. Surely a gift is a good act, for whatever reason given, or whatever reason accepted? The act counts for more than the intention.

*

This radiant June afternoon was too self-sufficient and too self-contained to give anything to an onlooker, or to receive anything from him. Like a successful work of art, it basked in its own perfection.

Myra murmured something.

'I beg your pardon,' I said, and I meant it in more ways than one.

'I was thinking about this lovely day,' she said, 'and what a *gift* it is. Something one could never have thought of for oneself, because the essence of a gift is that it should be a surprise no, not a surprise—how silly I am! But it should bring the sense of *otherness*, which one can't give oneself, any more than one can shake hands with oneself. One *can*, of course; one can *wring* one's hands, but that's not the same thing. I've never done it, but I imagine it gives you a double dose of self-infiltration, as if you had a looking-glass on both sides of you.'

'I suppose that would be bliss to a narcissist,' I said, 'to be yourself duplicated, triplicated, and even quadrupled! But as you say, it wouldn't give the sense of *otherness*. Only someone else can give that, or withhold it. Do you like the sense of otherness, Myra? Not everybody does.'

We had done another double bend down to the plain before she answered.

'I think I know what you mean,' she said. 'We were going to talk about it, weren't we—the Girtin? It would be a sort of two-fold gift, from you and from him—from Gilbert.'

'And from Aunt Clare,' I said. 'That makes three.'

Myra agreed. 'Do you know,' she said, 'I sometimes wish that Aunt Clare had left anything she wanted me to have, to me, direct? As she did to her husband's relations. But the things she left to Gilbert'—her voice died out. 'It must have been hard for him to make up his mind.'

'Oh, I don't know,' I said. 'He had only to make a list.'

'And I didn't figure on it? Well, I haven't yet.'

'Well, you have now,' I said. 'That is, if you like the Girtin.'

'I like it, but I don't like to rob you of it,' she said, troubled. 'It is such a pretty thing, a darling. You will miss it, I'm afraid, and I have plenty of pictures.'

'Still, it was his wish,' I sighed. The sigh was partly for myself, and the role I was playing. 'He told you so, didn't he?' I felt I must risk this.

Myra hesitated.

'Not quite in so many words. He said he had never felt sure

84

the picture would suit me, was *me*, as they say. Perhaps he had said something to you about it, but he couldn't exactly remember, because it was so long since he saw you. You haven't quarrelled, have you?' she asked me suddenly.

'Not that I know of,' I replied. 'But I haven't seen him for—for several weeks.'

'You used to be such great friends,' mused Myra. 'And there were some other friends of his—I can't remember who, who told me they hadn't seen him for some time.'

'Had he given them anything of Aunt Clare's?'

'Yes, because I remember them saying they ought to give some kind of party for him, and would I join in, and I said I couldn't because he hadn't given me anything. It was a little embarrassing.'

'What did they say to that?'

'They seemed surprised, and said the party must wait until I had received my benefaction.' Myra laughed a little.

'When was that?' I asked.

'Oh, quite a time ago.'

'How odd,' I said. 'I expect he has been working.'

'But it's when he's working that he most wants to see his friends,' observed Myra. 'I suppose they help to give him back what he puts into his music.'

'I rather doubt that,' I replied. 'His friends—if I can still count myself one,—don't give him back the sort of things he puts into his music. At least I don't, and I should be surprised if you did, Myra. When did *you* last see him?' I made it sound an accusation.

'I dined with him the day before I came out here.'

'Oh you did, did you?' I exclaimed. 'What comment did he make, if any, about your going to Assisi?'

'I've such a bad verbal memory,' said Myra, with a touch of resentment. 'I think he did say it would be fun for me your being out here, too.'

'Oh, so he knew I was here? Somebody must have told him.'

'Why didn't you tell him yourself?'

'I have a bad verbal memory,' I retorted, 'and it's so long since I saw him. I doubt if he remembers me. I live on my grateful recollections of his friendship, symbolized by the Girtin.'

'He was never one for giving presents,' Myra mused. 'Almost less than anyone I know. I know that sounds unkind but it's the truth. He may have had some kink, and thought that present-giving injures friendship.'

'He seems to have been right in his own case,' I said. 'You are the only one of his friends, so far as I know, who remains on the old footing with him.'

'You forget Barbara. Did he give Barbara anything?'

'Yes, a pretty Crown Derby teapot.'

'That wasn't very much.'

'No. And does he still see her?' I asked.

'What an inquisitor you are,' laughed Myra. 'Yes, I should think so, because he relies on her to copy out his music. No one else can read these squiggles.'

'Does he pay her for it?'

'Yes, I fancy so. Does it matter?'

'It may have started something in him,' I said. 'And remember that he hadn't the wherewithal for present-giving until his aunt died. His music doesn't bring in very much, and he had next to nothing of his own until she gave him a modicum of money. The *objets* came later. Whether she wanted him to distribute them, we shall never know. At least I shan't, *you* may.'

'Why I, more than anyone else?' asked Myra.

'Because you still enjoy his friendship and his confidence.'

'If I do,' said Myra, 'isn't it rather odd that he never gave me one of Poor Clare's keepsakes?'

'Now you're asking.'

'And then suggested you should give me yours. If I didn't know how truthful you were, Edward, I should find that story hard to believe.'

'But he didn't deny it, did he?'

'No, in the circumstances he hardly could. But as I told you, he seemed a little taken aback.'

'Did he bring the subject up when you last saw him, the day before yesterday?'

Myra hesitated.

'Yes, he did. He asked me if you had brought or sent the picture round to me. When I said no, he seemed rather relieved.'

'What else did he say?'

'He said he would like to talk to you about it. And when I reminded him that he couldn't, because you were here, he talked of coming here himself, to make a shadowy third, as he put it.'

I was dumbfounded by this, though I had myself proposed it.

'Well, it will be very nice to see him,' I said at last, 'though I can't flatter myself that *I* shall be the object of his visit. And now, dear Myra,' I said more briskly, 'would you like a siesta' (we had lunched in Perugia) 'or would you like to do some sight-seeing? I usually work in the morning, but today has been a *dies non*, thanks to your presence. If you come with me to Santa Chiara, you could look at the church I am trying to paint, and visit San Francesco on your way back to our hotel. Downhill all the way! But as it's so hot, and I have my gear to carry, I generally take a taxi up to the church. What about it?'

I felt rather mean about making this arrangement, but work is work and always suffers from interruptions.

*

Myra waited to see me installed on my painting post, wedged between two taxis in the rank opposite the church. Here, almost facing it, I had an excellent view of the buttresses, which sprang from the ground and seemed almost literally to fly to meet the beautiful octagonal pilasters which helped to support the roof. Now that Myra was with me, my painting seemed to have taken on a new lease of life: it soared with the buttresses and suddenly I could achieve the extra definition, the hardness of outline, that the Italian sunlight requires. Besides the buttresses, there were many things to define—the alternate lateral lines of pink and white stone that swept across the façade, the broader, more pronounced line that divided the great round-headed doorway from

the magnificent rose-window above; the second line that pro-
jected over the window, and formed the base of the unflinching,
geometrically perfect triangle, broken only by a small round
window, behind which, invisible from where I sat, lay the roof.

One could not call it simple but it was marvellously simplified,
both in design and execution; none of the doubts and hesitations
which beset the English landscape, be it trees or hills or buildings,
and thus beset the painter. Under the Italian sky all was plain
sailing, for the artist, as it should be for the man.

As it should be and as it would be.

For why should Gilbert have kept Myra on a string for all
these years, knowing that she would never marry anyone else
while he was still free? Anyone, no matter whom, me, for
instance? He must have suspected that I loved her, but this had
never invalidated our friendship, his and mine. I was always
fond of him, and his behaviour to Myra was after all his business;
if we had changed places, he would not, I felt sure, have thought
the worse of me for not marrying Myra. In our circle we thought
we behaved in such matters as civilized human beings. Many of
us believed that Myra was, or had been Gilbert's mistress, but no
one knew, and I was perhaps the only one who hoped that she
had not.

Now that I had her with me the situation could surely be
clarified, just as the sunshine clarified the lines and angles of the
West Front of Santa Chiara's church. Would Myra have come
to Assisi if her heart was still with Gilbert? I didn't think so, and
I wouldn't let my feeling of loyalty to him interfere with what
was best for Myra and me. I felt that not only had I starved my
visual sense by accepting the indeterminate aspect of the English
scene; I had starved my other senses too. Now, thanks to Santa
Chiara's inspiration, I should pursue a more clear-cut and a more
objective course.

Chapter Twelve

THE days passed. I finished my picture of Santa Chiara, and almost, but not quite, hand in hand with Myra (for people in their middle forties do not in England walk hand in hand) I searched for a new subject. The roofs of Assisi are fascinating: I wanted my new subject to include its criss-cross roofs. For that we had to go uphill. It was too hot to climb on foot, so eventually we took a taxi up the newly metalled road which leads to the Rocca Maggiore, the huge ruined castle that overhangs Assisi from the summit of the hill. There, beneath the great round bastion which had been occupied by, among many other war-lords, Frederick Barbarossa, we found the ideal view-point. Ideal in every way, because not only did it command the roofs and domes and towers of the town, but it also gave, in a south-westerly direction, the façade and buttresses of Santa Chiara, far below, and higher up, and flanking it, the West Front of the Cathedral of San Rufino, with its magnificent romanesque campanile and the grey-blue dome behind it. The two façades were remarkably similar although San Rufino's was the richer and I suppose the older: but they repeated each other like phrases in music; by re-echoing they enhanced each other, both by their likenesses and their differences. One had three doors instead of one, three rose windows instead of one, and a much higher gable, with an arch inset. San Rufino perhaps did not aim at the austerity and simplicity which were such marked features of St. Clare's. The Cathedral was much darker in tone as well as more elaborate in ornament, but together, seen from above, they had a compositional value which neither would have had singly, and the complex pattern of the flat-pitched, grey roofs, with their pinkish tinge, almost lilac in certain lights, spread under, around and beyond them, gave them the eminence and pre-eminence which they needed.

The scene was a symphony, not a solo, as my portrait of Santa Chiara had been: it would and did take much longer.

Sometimes we had a sandwich lunch in whatever shade we could find, for shade was hard to come by except under the vast curtain-wall of the Castle. But often I came alone, leaving Myra to explore and sightsee, for it was dull for her to sit watching me, and much as I delighted in her company, I never liked an on-looker while I was painting, dear as she was.

Increasingly dear; but though I knew my own mind I did not know hers, and had no way of finding out except by asking her. And this I could not bring myself to do. I dared not put it to the touch to win or lose it all, and everyday I found an excuse for postponing it. Sometimes I told myself I would 'put her in the picture' (as they say) when I had finished this or that passage in *my* picture, but a donkey cannot provide himself with carrots, and I didn't, and perhaps I never should have if she had not announced, quite casually and unexpectedly, that in a few days she must be getting back to London.

'Must you?' I exclaimed.

'*Must* you?' I repeated, 'I hoped you were going to stay—oh, quite a long time.'

'I'm afraid I must,' she said. 'I've had a lovely holiday and it's been the greatest fun, but I have things to see to, and people to see, in London.'

'Such as?' I asked.

'Oh tiresome things you wouldn't know about. They aren't important but they need attention, and you can't count on the post here.'

'Have you had any letters?' I asked suspiciously.

'Yes, one or two.'

'Have you heard from Gilbert? Because I haven't.'

'Yes. I had a letter from him this morning.'

'And is that why you decided to go home?'

'Dear Edward, what a lot of questions you ask! You are a real nosey-parker. He's not getting on well with his symphony. He says he's lonely.'

'But if he is, whose fault is that? He has deliberately avoided us it seems to me—all of us except you, and Barbara, who doesn't really count. Ever since, ever since—'

'Ever since he gave away those things of his aunt's,' Myra broke in. 'I wonder if that bequest did him any good. He wasn't fitted for it somehow—psychologically, I mean.'

'What do you mean?'

'I mean that he lives in his music and isn't at all practical. The legacy and what to do about it knocked him sideways—he hasn't been the same man since.'

'How do you know all this?'

'He told me how much it had upset him, thinking what he ought to do, and so on. He has more sense of responsibility than you might imagine.'

'I know he *had*,' I said, and for a moment the feeling of my friendship with Gilbert came back in full force. But that was only friendship and this, I reminded myself, was love.

'Did he mention me in his letter?'

'There you go again!' said Myra tolerantly. 'Yes, Edward, he did.'

'What did he say?'

Myra hesitated.

'He asked me to give you his love and tell you he had changed his mind about the picture.'

'What picture?'

'The Girtin. He said he didn't want you to give it me, because he had something else he wanted to give me.'

'Did he say what?'

'No, but he said he would tell me when I got back.'

I was thunderstruck by this, and by the ease with which Gilbert had countered my little plot.

'I don't believe he wants to give you *anything!*' I burst out. 'If he had, surely he would have given it you before, and not waited until I'—I couldn't finish the sentence.

'Until you?'—prompted Myra gently.

'Until I—until we were together, until I had you to myself.'

Myra turned away and looked at the dark plain, now star-sprinkled with lights. She said nothing.

'Listen, Myra,' I begged. 'I know that Gilbert is my friend, and a very good friend he has been too, until just lately. But he has always stood between me and you. You have sacrificed yourself to him and to . . . to the fulfilment of his talent, as only a woman could—perhaps as only you could. You have loved him, I know, and perhaps he loves you because—let me speak frankly —you were necessary to him. I don't believe he loved you for yourself as I do, and have done for many years, as he himself must know, unless his nature is as discordant, as deaf to any outside harmony, as his music is. Whatever part of him his music comes from, it isn't love—it *sounds* much more like hatred —and he only keeps you by him because somehow you are able to maintain him in his creative mood. No, please, Myra,' for she had made a gesture of dissent or protest—'don't let him go on feeding on you, as if you were some sort of emotional vitamin— you are too good for that. Don't let him be your parasite, because he'll drain you dry, I know he will!'

I stopped, bewildered, apprehensive, but relieved by having said at last what I had so long wanted to say.

Myra, who had been listening with averted head at last turned to me, her face almost unrecognizable from the concourse of emotions which possessed it.

'Then what do you advise me to do?' she said at last.

I was still under the intoxication of my own outspokenness.

'How can you ask? Why, marry me, of course.'

She nodded gravely, as if this was the answer she had been expecting.

'But supposing I don't love you?'

'You could come to!' I urged. 'You must like me a little, or you wouldn't have come out here to join me.'

She nodded again, not, so it seemed, to me, but as if in confirmation of her own thoughts. She said, choosing her words.

'Of course I like you, but liking isn't the same as love.'

'And you love Gilbert?'

She moved her head from side to side.

'Yes, I think I do, perhaps not as much as I once did . . . You see, he has always needed me, and he needs me still.'

'But needing you is not enough,' I cried. 'It's a matter of your giving and his taking. Couldn't you take something as well as give it, Myra? Besides, I need you, too. Think how much easier it has been for me to paint since you were here! You yourself said I was painting better, and you must have known why! But my art is from my life a thing apart, 'tis Gilbert's whole existence! I don't like his work as much as I like him, but I grant he is a more important artist than I shall ever be.'

'I don't know about that,' said Myra. 'I think you underrate yourself, you always have. But you have come to terms with life, and Gilbert hasn't.'

'There!' I said, 'you see. You admit that you, with all your devotion to him, haven't brought him to come to terms with life, and you never will! He'll use you, just as he always has, as a means of keeping life at bay, while he writes all that chaotic, life-destroying stuff, which is about as much like art as a town hit by an atom-bomb! Without you,' I said, 'he might have calmed down, and written decent, ordinary music. It's you who keeps him at the pitch of frenzy, and by fending off other influences, let him gesticulate in his own vacuum!'

'You said you were a friend of his,' said Myra. 'You don't talk as if you were.'

The remembrance of Gilbert's friendship again swept across my mind and I was conscience-stricken.

'No, no, all I meant was that by protecting him with the golden halo of your good-will you have encouraged him to be more himself than it is good for any artist to be. Whereas with me—'

'What could I do for you?' asked Myra.

'Well, you could criticize me. I need criticism, and the sense of other people's thoughts working on mine, almost as much as

Gilbert needs unqualified approval. And perhaps I could do something for you, too.'

'What could you do for me?'

'I could give you, at least I hope I could, a sense of being loved and treasured for yourself, as every woman has a right to be. Don't tell me you don't want that, Myra, and that you would rather be the moon, with only one side that the sun reflects, and that not always, than an independent luminary showing us, showing me, whatever aspect of yourself you choose to show? And remember this, I have always given other people's emotions priority to mine. There is always a hundredth chance of happiness —do you want to shut the door on that?'

Myra's trembling lips betrayed her agitation. Hastily and clumsily she made them up, looking at me from under her brows as if I were some kind of mirror. Suddenly all the lights on the terrace went out, and we could only see each other by the glow reflected from the lights in the valley.

'They want us to go,' said Myra in a low, troubled voice. 'I'll think over what you said, Edward. Thank you for saying it. Perhaps my mind will be clearer in the morning. Goodnight,' and without another word she left me.

'Myra!' I called into the darkness, but she did not come back.

Chapter Thirteen

A WEEK later we were still at Assisi, that was the only fact I had to build on, for Myra had become a little remote and withdrawn. She accompanied me less frequently on my painting sessions, but made excursions on her own to neighbouring places; Gubbio, Spoleto, Orvieto, and so on. Once or twice she asked me to go with her; but more often she said she wouldn't, because she didn't want to disturb me at my painting.

Whether her mind was made up, or even clearer, she didn't tell me and I didn't ask her; I left it to her to re-open the subject. I couldn't say any more: I had laid my cards on the table and it was her turn to play. I imagined that she had written to Gilbert, for she always answered letters promptly.

Meanwhile I had finished my picture of the two West Fronts, rising above the petrified sea of roofs, which, from above, seemed one solid mass, with no room for the streets between them.

I liked the picture and Myra liked it, too. 'It has got so much depth and feeling in it,' she said, 'and I like the two churches balancing each other—two are better than one. Are they symbolic of anything, do you think? Santa Chiara, in the distance, is very like St. Clare, and not unlike Gilbert's Aunt Clare, for that matter. That tall, stiff campanile with its pepper-pot spire would serve for either of them. But San Rufino—I don't know—I must find out more about him. You have brought out the male and female quality in each of them—San Rufino sombre and almost lowering, Santa Chiara light and almost smiling, yet both so much alike. Would it be irreverent to imagine a marriage between churches? Or if not a marriage, a respectful and affectionate relationship? At a distance, of course, a quarter of a mile, perhaps.'

I wondered what Myra was driving at.

'I can see several likenesses in St. Clare's Church,' I said, 'and Myra, you are one. But San Rufino doesn't represent any one I know. Certainly not me. Outside, it has a look of Gilbert, or rather of Gilbert's mind, dark and inscrutable and defiant; but inside, all that richness, that multi-coloured marble, that baroque coating to what must once have been a plain Romanesque church—no, I don't see Gilbert like that.'

'Your thoughts still run on Gilbert,' Myra said.

'Yes, and do yours?'

'We had to come to that sometime,' Myra said. 'I have written to him, of course—have you, Edward?'

'Not since you came.'

'I see myself as the villain of the piece, or as the co-villain. I won't deny Edward, that I was moved and touched, flattered and gratified, by what you told me. You said your life would be complete if we were together. Well, so would mine be. But there is the fact that I do love him. I don't know if he loves me, but he depends on me in a way you never could. You could give me what he can't or doesn't—but feeling as I still do for him, what could I give you?'

'I've told you,' I said. 'Everything.'

'And you wouldn't feel that I was being disloyal, or that you were?'

'Of course I should, Myra,' I said, 'and no doubt you would too. But can anything worth while be got without sacrifice, and very often without the sacrifice of a principle that you cherish? There is no romance without withholding, but morality was made for man, not man for morality. In your case, I know, it wouldn't be so much sacrificing a principle as sacrificing—well, love; a much more vital objection than the bad conscience of a cad, which I should have. But we all owe life a debt, without which we shouldn't be alive,—for I don't suppose that either of us was conceived and born to satisfy a moral principle.'

'But equally not in defiance of a moral principle,' Myra said.

'Presumably not, but we aren't to know that. But I do feel that in the sphere of personal relations into which crime doesn't enter, life has its claims which cannot be ignored.'

Myra was silent for a while and then she said:

'But what about these gifts, Edward? Don't they put us all under an obligation to Gilbert? Even supposing his aunt asked him to distribute them, which we shall never know, we are still his debtors, and not only materially, but emotionally.'

'But he hasn't given you anything,' I said rashly.

'You told me he wanted me to have your Girtin, Edward. Was that true?'

I hung my head and looked the other way.

'No, it wasn't.'

Most men would have been angry at this disclosure, but Myra only said, 'I had an idea it wasn't. But why did you make up that story, Edward?'

I explained my theory about Gilbert's prize-givings, and ended up, 'He discarded the rest of us, don't you see, he paid us off. But he didn't give you anything, because he wanted to keep you by him.'

It was a shabby, sorry story, and came out haltingly. I felt a little better, morally, for having made a clean breast of it but I felt a fool and worse for having been trapped, or having trapped myself, into telling it.

But Myra, to my surprise, didn't seem to think the worse of me.

'What an ingenious plot!' she said. 'I didn't think you had it in you, Edward. Of course, I can't help feeling flattered, but really you were very, very naughty. I only half believed you, though.'

'Why didn't you believe me?' I asked, inexpressibly relieved.

'Well, it seemed such an odd thing for Gilbert to do—to want you to give me the present he had given you. It simply isn't done, is it, at least not in our circles. And then his saying he had changed his mind, and wanted to give me something else—well, that almost convinced me that you had trumped the story up. Is he a glutton for gratitude, do you think?'

'It doesn't look like it,' I said. 'He hasn't given me much chance to show my thanks.'

'It's a very subtle way of undermining a friendship,' Myra said, 'to give someone a present one knows they can't return, for gratitude is a burden on most friendships. I wonder what he thinks of giving me?'

'I've no idea,' I answered, rather shortly. 'A token present, I should think. Nothing you could be grateful for.'

'Nothing concrete?'

'No.'

'What, then?'

'I haven't a clue.'

Myra was silent for a time, and we looked upwards at the Rocca Maggiore, the great castle, which was the new subject of my brush, a mountain of pale grey masonry, making a rough triangle, of which the tower of the keep formed the apex, and the two curtain walls stretching away on either side, the base. I wished I could have included the whole of the much longer and more impressive wall that extended for a hundred yards to the left and ended in a decagonal tower crowned with another, smaller and hexagonal in shape, a most satisfying design, but it wouldn't fit into my scheme. Perhaps I could paint the tower by itself, later.

Topographically, the position was almost the same as the one from which I had painted the two churches: one turned one's back on the other view, and one's face to this one. I had bought two light canvas chairs and a four-legged stool with a board on top, to which I pinned my drawing-paper. Altogether it was quite a load, and I used to ask the driver who brought us, or me, up, to come again in two or three hours' time. It was a stiff climb to the Rocca, four or five hundred feet above our hotel. When I was alone I sometimes stopped painting and walked along the level path to the solitary tower. The path was an irregular convex curve, skirting the top of the hill, with the town nestling below and the plain stretching all the way round: it commanded one of the most spectacular views in Italy. The plain was divided as far as the eye could see by a straight road to the north-west, which, when the afternoon sun caught it, shone like a river.

Myra said: 'I must write to Gilbert, but I don't know how to put it.'

My heart leapt; she had made up her mind at last.

'Perhaps I should write to him, too,' I said cautiously.

'But it will be difficult,' she went on. 'It may upset him and give him a shock, the sort of shock his music is so full of.'

My conscience pricked me as I said, 'I don't suppose he'll mind all that much.' But I hardened my heart; what was one short shock, however sharp, compared to the years of devoted but frustrated service that Myra had lavished on him?

'It won't be so hard for me,' I said, 'as it would have been a few weeks ago, before he—he broke off his friendship with me. Then, I couldn't have done it. But now it will be almost like writing to a stranger.'

'But not for me,' she answered. 'For me it will be, oh, . . . don't let's talk about it, Edward.'

'But you will write, won't you?' I begged. 'And then I'll post our letters both together.'

'I'll try but I don't promise,' she said and to my horror she began to cry. 'Bring my chair with you, please,' she said, rising abruptly. 'I'm going to walk down.'

*

I had my letter ready.

Dear Gilbert,

It is difficult to write a letter when you don't know what its effect will be. I try to think that mine, and Myra's will bring you, if not happiness, at any rate the peace of mind for which you have always striven. You were once a great friend of mine, and I can't say how much I valued your friendship. But latterly it has seemed to me that you no longer needed my friendship; and the exquisite Girtin, for which I shall always be grateful, was a kind of substitute, a concrete substitute for friendship, a parting gift. I am not alone in feeling this: other friends of yours, have also felt that your marvellous generosity has been as it were a full-stop to friendship. I won't say you don't any longer want us, but you don't need us and would rather be without us—it is like the changes of mood that happens so dramatically in your music.

People, those other friends of yours, have said, cynically, 'It would have been natural for us to drop Gilbert, when we have all been "bunched" with bouquets, so to speak, and have nothing more to get out of him; but why should *he* drop *us*?' I think I know the explanation. Perhaps I have already told you. For some reason you want to get rid of us, and have chosen this way of giving us our *congé*. I must say it was a very delicate and generous way to dismiss us all with a blessing—all except Myra. Did we represent the discords in your music? Or were we an obstacle to them?

You live in a world of fantasy in which symbols count for more than thoughts or even feelings. At least that's how I interpret it, and I think how Myra interprets it. I have loved her for many years, as I think she has loved you, but now we have both come to feel the need of a stronger and more direct relationship than can be symbolized by gifts however precious. What you have given me, and may be going to give Myra, is a challenge to gratitude that we can't accept, for it would come between us and our feelings for each other. Grateful we shall always be, and gratitude is a bond, but not so strong a bond as the ordinary natural love of one person for another.'

I tore this up and started again.

Dear Gilbert,

I am writing to tell you that Myra and I have decided to get married. I hope this won't come as a blow to you. It would be stupid of me to pretend not to know how close you and she were to each other, or for how many years, but I hope she will not cease to be an inspiration to you, just because she is a comfort, and much more than a comfort, to me. To me she will be *everything*. I may be wrong, but to you I don't think she was ever more than a beautiful landscape is to me. Forgive me if I have hurt you, dear Gilbert. Think of us both as happy, and we shall try to think of you, to whom we owe so much, as not unhappy.

With my love,

Edward.

I showed Myra the letter and she seemed to approve of it, but there was something guarded in her approval and I spent part of my painting time devising other versions of it, though I did not submit them to her. Time suddenly became important to me—the passage of time, the days of the week; I ticked them off.

Is your letter ready, Myra?

Is your letter ready, Myra?

Is your letter ready, Myra?—

And always each time she answered, 'Not quite ready, I'll tell you when it is.'

*

I don't remember how long this went on; it wasted some of the time and energy I needed for my picture of the Rocca. The Rocca was there for me to see, the same Rocca as it had been for centuries, with its walls and the tufts of vegetation sprouting high up on its walls; whereas my mood in looking at it changed continually. Art is a jealous mistress, but so is life; neither will tolerate divided loyalties; each must come first. This I knew but it was no help to me, nor was it any help to remember that many artists had been able to combine the emotions that life and art demand.

'Is your letter ready, Myra?'

I tried to put the question as casually as I could, and at different times of day, so as not to make it seem automatic, and I altered the phrasing, even trying to make it sound facetious, 'How goes your correspondence, Myra? Any news for me today? Any outgoing mail?' For I was determined that my letter shouldn't go without hers to back it up.

Chapter Fourteen

How long this deadlock might have lasted I cannot say. I refused to be discouraged by it: I kept telling myself that Myra's mind was really made up, and the only reason why she hesitated was because, as I did, she found it hard to find the right words to break the news to Gilbert. Every morning I awoke full of hope that today, at last, I should take the two letters to the red post-box at the far end of the Piazza del Comune, for I did not mean to trust them to the hotel staff.

Myra didn't come down very early, sometimes not until half-past ten, and very often I would wait beside the lift till it disgorged her, hoping she would have the letter in her hand. She wouldn't have had, of course; the letter would have been in her bag: she wouldn't have advertised it, she might have wanted to keep its presence hidden even from herself. Optimistically I tried to think she had posted it without telling me and that one day she would say, 'I know why you are hanging about here; well, you needn't any more,'—with such a laughing face that all the long days of waiting would seem as if they had been wiped out by a smile.

The incoming post had very little interest for me. I didn't write more letters than I could help, and my correspondents did not always answer them: when people are abroad their existence becomes dim and almost fabulous: why bother to write a letter when it may never reach them? No one will ever forward it; to write it will be a waste of time. The letters I had received while I was at Assisi could have been counted on the fingers of one hand.

One day while I was waiting for Myra, walking up and down, pretending to look at the murals of exotic scenes, the half-naked ladies and gentlemen courting each other under palm-trees, meant to entice visitors to stay at Assisi, a waiter came up to me. What does he want? I thought; have I transgressed some by-law of the place, failed to fill in some form as a result of which I shall be instantly expelled?—for my mind turns readily to guilty thoughts, especially where official regulations are concerned. The man bowed: 'Signor Eduardo?' he asked, for by this time I had come to be known by my Christian name—my surname was too harsh for an Italian tongue. 'Una lettera per lei,' and he handed me an envelope.

I knew the handwriting: it was Barbara's. I hadn't heard from her and had seldom thought of her, since I came to Assisi. Once she had meant a great deal to me, and I to her, but that was years ago, before Myra had eclipsed her image in my mind. Since she had become Gilbert's secretary he no doubt meant more to her than I did. She was as forthright as Myra was non-committal, she didn't mince her words: she hadn't when I asked her to give Gilbert the false message about the Girtin. That episode hadn't made a breach between us, but I could see it had lowered me in her regard and would, no doubt, have lowered me in my own if I hadn't thought that the conquest of Myra demanded a relaxation of my moral standards.

Her handwriting brought back a crowd of memories of the life I had led before Assisi. They had been submerged years ago; but now they came to the surface, fragmentary reminders of an old affection and the familiarity for which, as one grows older, there is no substitute. All the same, I viewed the fat envelope with some apprehension.

'Dear Edward,' she wrote, 'I have been wanting to write to you for a long time, ever since you went away, indeed—how long ago that seems! But I didn't want to worry you with letters which might distract you from your work—for I know how all-important that is to you. And I wouldn't have written now, if I hadn't thought that there is something that you ought to know. Such an alarming phrase—but don't be alarmed, it isn't serious, at least I don't think it is. And please don't imagine that we have been discussing you, and wondering about your holiday with Myra, because it's no business of mine or ours: my only wish is, as it always has been, for you to be happy and go your own way without others butting in.

But I think I ought to tell you that since you went away Gilbert has changed, changed in a way I can't easily describe. To say he has had a nervous breakdown would be too strong, but he has certainly shown some of the symptoms. He is no longer the mouse-like creature, outside if not inside, that he used to be,—it was almost a by-word, wasn't it, the contrast between him and his music. People simply couldn't believe when they met him, that he was the composer of the *Sinfonia Disorientata*. Now all that has changed. Even to look at, he's like a mouse on its hind legs. He has flashes of irritability, even with me, when I can't read his strange musical script which is so full of erasures that there is more to leave out than to leave in. He complains of trifles and above all he complains of not being able to finish his *Cantata per i Perduti*. That isn't a trifle, of course, but all this grumbling makes him an uncomfortable companion, and so unlike his old self, for he has lost the sense of humour which used to make his antics funny. It is as though he was trying to make up for years of self-suppression by taking it out of whoever happens to be nearest, which is generally me, for he hardly sees anything of his old friends.

I see a great deal of him in the course of copying out his music, a job I used to love. But I daily find it more difficult, for not only is his notation more indecipherable than it once was, but he is always re-writing what he has written. I think he regrets having given me his aunt's teapot and would like it back! He now calls it 'loot' and I think the problem of distributing the loot has been more of a mental and nervous strain than he will admit. A little while ago he said he wished 'Poor Clare' had kept her poverty to herself, and when I said she couldn't because you can't take poverty with you any more than you can riches, he only grunted and said there are other ways of killing a cat than by choking it with cream.

When we are together he talks a lot about Myra, and says he can't understand why she stays away so long when she must know that he can't work properly without her. Whatever else I am, I am certainly not his Muse! He accuses you of selfishness and sometimes says he will go to Assisi and break up your idyll, and carry Myra off by force!! Of course he doesn't mean that—he has always said things he doesn't mean—and sometimes (this is between ourselves) he seems to mix up his Aunt Clare with Saint Clare, though no two human beings (if a saint is a human being) could be less alike—except that they each lived for a principle, I suppose, and left bequests to benefit posterity. He even said that he would like to see Saint Clare mummified on her tomb (which you no doubt have seen) because it might help him to understand his Aunt Clare better! Such fancy notions, and rather morbid too, I think.

I'm not happy about him, I don't think he is well, either physically or mentally, he certainly doesn't *look* well and I have urged him to go away somewhere, for the sake of the change, though *not* to Assisi! But he won't. He still thinks that Myra ought to come back to him.

Now this is no business of mine, Edward, but Gilbert is, or has been, very dear to us all, and I hate to see him going downhill in the way he obviously is now. I hope and think you are having a wonderful time in Assisi, I know that you will be working better with Myra about (she can help artists in a way I never could), but without appealing too much to our old friendship (which is still a precious memory to me) may I suggest that you drop a hint to Myra,—not making out Gilbert's condition's worse than it is—to come back? It would be a sacrifice, for I know you are devoted to her, as we all are, but it would be a blessing to Gilbert, and save him from I don't quite know what. Will you do this?

When I think of our long four-sided relationship, I sometimes wonder how it appears to the outside world. Four human beings, two men and two women, all attached to each other for a number of years, and yet not one marriage, I don't count mine, whereas by today's standards there might have been at least twelve, three for each of us, and perhaps a child or two between us. Would it have been better that way? It would certainly have been more fashionable, and I can't pretend I'm not influenced by fashion. But would it have been *better*? I can't define the word. We should have looked more satisfactory, as adult human beings than we look now—an unmarried childless quartet, loving each other, but not enough, disagreeing with each other, but not enough, agreeing with each other, but not enough, and what to show for it? Your painting, Gilbert's music, Myra's elegant life among her elegant belongings, and my—what shall I say? Perhaps the less said about me, the better. It doesn't amount to much, does it, that I am Gilbert's drudge?

But I'm sure you won't misunderstand me when I say that if we could have had a justification, a quadripartite justification, if there is such a thing, it would have been Gilbert's happiness and success. That he hasn't had either isn't our fault, we have done our best, Myra has done her best, but he has turned out to be a *mauvais sujet,* a miniscule Beethoven without the genius. He is 45, as we all are, more or less, but I still think he has it in him to do something worth while—*if only Myra would come back!* We have all been critical of him at one time or another; he has exasperated us without giving us much in return—except his aunt's treasures—they were an acknowledgment of obligation, I feel sure, but Myra didn't get one. Why not, Edward why not? It's an academic question, I'm not a gold-digger any more than Myra is (she has no need to be), but why must we suppose that Poor Clare, *via* Gilbert, didn't have her in mind?

But however she phrased her will she *did* have Gilbert in mind; she believed in him and in his talent, and perhaps she wanted to give him greater confidence in himself by making over to him all those nice things. She didn't get much out of them herself, but she thought they would add to Gilbert's stature. Apparently they haven't, they've done the opposite, owing to some complex psychological trauma, which would only have happened to a man like him. Myra is the key to it all, *she* can unlock the door, and I *beseech* you, Edward, I *implore* you, to *send her packing,* lest a worse thing should befall. You have listened to me in the past; please listen to me now.

With all my love,

Barbara.

While I was re-reading Barbara's letter, I heard a footstep and felt the impress of a shadow coming over me. I looked up: it was Myra. She was holding something in her hand.

'Haven't you gone out yet, lazy-bones?' she asked. 'I was so late, I was afraid I should have missed you. I am so glad I didn't, because now you can post a letter for me. Or we can post it together, if you would like me to go with you to the Rocca.'

'I have one, too,' I said, taking out an envelope—rather battered from much friction in my pocket. 'Are they addressed to the same person?'

'I'm not sure. I want you to see who mine is addressed to,' said Myra, taking it from her bag.

'I could say the same,' I said, and laid my letter beside hers on the table.

Gilbert's name was on each envelope. 'I wonder if they will be travelling-companions,' I said, 'or if they will get separated. The Italian post is so erratic. I would rather they arrived together— that is, if your letter says the same as mine does.'

'It says what you asked me to say,' said Myra. 'I think it was my sixth attempt, but I'm not proud of it.'

'It was my seventh,' I said, 'and I'm not proud of it, either. But in this case, darling, it isn't the manner of the wooing that matters, it's the match.'

We kissed each other. I was lost to anything else. It was the first time in my life that I felt the totality of this or any re-lationship. No one who has ever experienced it can fail to know what it means, just as no one who has not experienced it can ever know. The place we were in had as little reality as the setting of a dream. When I came to myself I was aware of chairs and tables that I had known for weeks, with the same surprise and sense of estrangement as if they had been brought in that minute from a furniture store. Then they all resumed their identities and I resumed mine. I couldn't tell whether Myra had had a similar experience, but from the way she looked, like a diver surfacing, I thought she must have had.

My hand held hers. There was nothing to say, yet the silence between us had to be broken some time.

'Did you have any letters this morning?' she asked.

I cast my mind forwards and back.

'No . . . Oh yes, I had one.'

'Was it interesting, my darling?'

I realized that Myra did not care whether it was interesting or not; she was just feeling her way to a medium of verbal communication.

'No . . . yes . . . it was interesting in a way.' I could now feel Barbara's letter bulging, nay burning in my pocket.

Myra must have noticed my concern. 'Was it anything to do with us?'

'Oh no.'

'I only asked because you looked worried. It didn't bring bad news, I hope?'

'How could it, darling? There is no bad news now.' And I gave her another, longer kiss.

'Then shall we go to the Rocca? We can stop at the post-box on the way.'

Chapter Fifteen

THE world of imagination or the world of fact? The hero of my
own dream or the villain of Gilbert's? The reaction set in, as I
knew it would. I did no work that morning, or none that I didn't
wish undone. The world of the imagination is very different
from the world of fact. I suppose facts come from the imagination too, but they seem nearer to reality, the more disagreeable
they are. At times during the morning and in the days that
followed I was able to recapture the bliss of the moment when
Myra joined her letter to mine; but as the time drew nearer for
the letters to reach Gilbert (four days, five days, six days, seven
days?—one couldn't count, literally or metaphorically, on the
Italian post) my periods of uneasiness increased. I couldn't tell
if Myra also had them, for to outward appearance she was still
serene, as I suppose I was, so long as I was with her, for the
nearness of a beloved person has the power to banish fear, or
almost any emotion outside the magic touch. When alone I could
not give myself the reassurance, or, at times, not see myself
through Gilbert's and Barbara's, accusing eyes—a cad, a brute, a
viliaco, anything the language of his music liked to call me.

That feeling was strongest when I answered Barbara's letter.
I felt bound to answer it, it would have been cowardly not to,
and in sanguine moods I could still persuade myself that our
love, Myra's and mine, was its own justification. Why should I
feel morally more to blame than the thousands of other men who
had done just what I had? Again and again I told myself that one
can't make an omelette without breaking eggs, that morality is an
attitude of mind, 'a delicate sense of a variable custom' derived
from life, and couldn't exist without life, whereas life could
exist, and perhaps exist more happily without morality, and that

in any case the truest morality was to obey the dictates of one's being and stick to them. Besides, why should three people forgo their chances of happiness (for I didn't think that Barbara was very happy either) for the sake of one who had clearly shown that he was not happy himself or had the power, or the wish, to make other people happy? Some of this I tried to tell Barbara, with a pen that halted at every word, as if at a major road ahead,—almost, in my anxiety for self-justification, accusing her of meddling in other people's business. What was Gilbert to her, or I to her, that she should want to come between us and happiness?

One thing I told her, though it had little to do with the case, being an effort to externalize myself under the anonymous guise of a tourist, was that I hadn't seen the embalmed body of Saint Clare in the crypt of her church. I would do so at the earliest opportunity, for I, too, felt there was some affinity between the august foundress of the Order and the 'Poor Clare' we knew so little and had heard about so much, and whose gifts had almost founded an Order, the disorderly Order of Gilbert's many cast-off and his few remaining friends.

But I did not think I would take Myra with me.

Assisi is a happy town as befits the birthplace of St. Francis, one of the happiest and most rejoicing of the saints. Perhaps he bequeathed something of his spirit, though not its austerity, to the townsfolk, for they are always laughing and joking though not, to judge by appearances, working. They seem to live on air, with some help from picture-postcards, majolica ash-trays, bowls and jugs, beaten brass and copper ware, shirts and pullovers and dresses, often in blue and white, and designed for children or very small grown-ups. They sit on their doorsteps chatting, the women sewing, the men playing dominoes or cards; and when not so engaged they patrol the Piazza del Comune, nearly always with radiant carefree faces, and completely tolerant of the motor-cars, an ever-increasing menace, which creep up behind them noiselessly in the narrow paved streets and oblige them to jump sideways. Even the policeman in his white uniform has better things to do than directing traffic; he smiles and chats to the passers-by, exerting no authority because, seemingly, he has no need to. Are there no burglars, thugs, thieves, or other male-factors? Apparently not; for one cannot detect concealed ill-intent in those open, smiling faces. True, the downstairs windows are often barred, as in many Italian towns, but with ironwork so old and rusty it seems to have been designed to display the craftsman's skill rather than to keep out evil-doers.

And looking upwards, one sees the general joyousness flower-ing on the walls of the twisting streets, where balconies and circular iron stanchions and faded terra-cotta window-boxes are gay with geraniums and petunias, making a show which gladdens the heart, and is a source of so much pride to the inhabitants that every year the most notable exhibit wins a prize.

I did not go straight to Santa Chiara, I wandered up and down some of the streets I knew, for none is flat except for the piazza, and every destination has at least one alternative hill or flight of steps. Hundreds and hundreds of steps! Curling about, almost never straight, for there is scarcely a house in Assisi that stands at right-angles to its neighbour. I wanted to absorb the refresh-ment of the place, the light and air and genial hum of talk that bespeak a lasting alliance with and confidence in life.

All distances in Assisi seem short, not so much because the town itself is small, as because there is always a quicker way, if one knew which it was. St. Francis and St. Clare certainly knew the direct route but their fellow-townsmen in times to come took to paths that were topographically crooked but that got there in the end.

Such a path did I follow, on my way to Santa Chiara, an intentionally crooked path, a path as crooked as the one I had chosen for myself and Myra. Almost at every step it brought something new to look at, a humble doorway, a grand doorway, round-headed, peaked, or flat; no architectural feature was ever repeated; even the eves that sheltered them had their special dimension which threw its special shadow.

And so it will be with us, I thought, a winding of pleasant

ways, with always something to enchant the eye and the mind, instead of those monotonous straight tracks that we had worn through time, Myra towards an ideal that could not be fulfilled, I towards what? Following them we had cheated ourselves of the variousness of life.

Or so I thought, and let the richness of the visible scene keep other thoughts at bay. But one thought kept stinging me, like the mosquitoes from which even Assisi is not free, though they do not seem to worry its inhabitants. Of all the blights—the bad thoughts—that my relationship with Myra inspired when not exorcized by her presence—there was one particular gadfly which was always ready to sting. Unlike most of the others it was materialistic not moralistic. This gadfly was the present which, according to Barbara, Gilbert wanted to give Myra.

Myra was well off, much better off than I was, a fact which sometimes disturbed me, for people would think me a gold-digger as well as a traitor to my friend Gilbert. On the other hand, how could I bring myself to deprive her of a gift which might be really valuable, perhaps an Old Master or an Impressionist picture by a famous name? I had not disclosed to Myra any of the contents of Barbara's letter, I had not dared to. But supposing I was doing her out of a large sum of money? If she married me, I could not expect Gilbert to implement his promise, and give her whatever he had in mind for her,—as a wedding-present. He would be far too hurt and angry. He might even tell her, when he answered her letter if he did answer it— he was very bad at answering letters—what she was missing by throwing in her lot with me. I didn't think he would, but there was always the risk. I had taken full advantage of the proverb, 'All's fair in love and war', but there are limits, and Myra, who was sensitive to all sorts of imponderables, might feel I had overstepped the mark and have a revulsion for me. My per-suasions had tipped the balance in my favour, but only after days of pleading; one glance at me in the black guise in which I sometimes appeared to myself might alienate her for ever.

If I told her that Gilbert had something he wanted to give her she would ask me how I knew, and I should have to say, 'through Barbara', and then what might not come out? I couldn't say, 'Would you like to choose between me and Gilbert's potential gift?'—it would be too flat-footed, as stark as a Biblical story, and without the emotional force of a Biblical story, although so many Biblical stories turned on material matters, Jacob and Esau, for instance, in which Rebekah played a part as immoral as mine had been.

Chapter Sixteen

MY MOOD of elation cooled as I approached the familiar façade of Santa Chiara's church; I had looked at it so often, I had tried to do it justice in my picture, I respected it, I revered it, as an object of art and a symbol of religion. How far had we, or how far had I, fallen from grace since the time when it was built! No good thinking about that. I was more familiar with the outside than with the inside, although I knew fairly well its Gothic purity and the magnificent Crucifix behind its altar. But for some reason I had never ventured into the crypt, with its two entrances, one on each side of the choir, with, inscribed above them, ENTRATA and USCITA, Coming in and Going out—not from superstition or even from fear of superstition, but from a nameless feeling that here the special quality of Assisi, its manifestation of the goodness and happiness of life, might receive a shock.

Obediently I went down through the right-hand doorway, over which the word SILENZIO was ominously written; I went down some steps and turned leftwards: SILENZIO again. I went down further, and turned to the right, under another SILENZIO; there may have been a fourth turning, and another injunction to silence, before I came to the place I sought. It was all too strange—this approach through corridors of blue and white marble in the richest Victorian taste, until at last I stood before the grille behind which the saint lay. It was not an effigy, as I supposed; it was the veritable body of Santa Chiara, mummified or embalmed. She lay on a gorgeous gilded four-poster bed, in a black habit, with her face turned slightly towards me. The face was dark brown, but not the brown of any living creature; round her head a white mantle, decorated, if that be the word with (as far as I could see, peering) shells or flowers, or both. I realized that with me there was a company of other people, including several children; and within the grille, in the presence of the corpse, stood a nun, explaining, in several languages, who Santa Chiara was, and distributing leaflets, coloured leaflets, of the body on its gorgeous bed.

I looked a long time and then turned away. In front of me was a small staircase, again of the richest marble; I went up it, and there, behind another grille, was the simple grave, a plain dark, rectangular hole, with the thick stone slab, propped against the nearby wall, where the body had lain for six centuries, undiscovered.

In the dim light I saw a glittering on the flagstones between the grating and the grave, points of light as thick as stars in the sky. It came from hundreds of small nickel coins flung there by the faithful. I took a few out of my pocket and threw them through the bars.

It was a relief to be back in the church again and under its high vaulted roof instead of the dark cramped recesses of the crypt with its lively but awful occupant. All the same, I felt nearer to the presence of death, nearer to the fact of death, than I had ever done. All other facts seemed trivial by comparison, including my problems. It was a sobering experience and I walked back to the hotel, unaware of the bright sunshine, and not looking to the right hand or the left.

Chapter Seventeen

ON ARRIVING at the hotel I was told that while I was out there had been a telephone call for me.

'A telephone call!' I said. 'Who was it from?'

'A lady in London, signore. She did not give her name. She said she would ring you up again at one o'clock.'

One o'clock; it was now half-past twelve. Who could be ringing me up? I had written a few letters to friends on the hotel writing-paper, which had the telephone number printed on it. The caller might be one of several people. I tried to think who. I would have liked to discuss the possibilities with Myra, from whom, except for certain forbidden subjects, I had no secrets. But she was still out, sight-seeing.

She was not always on time for our usual one o'clock lunch, and my mind veered round: I began to hope that if the call came through (and the Italian telephone service was almost more unreliable than its post) it would come through before she came back. The telephone was in a public place: Myra was no eaves-dropper, but I hate to have my telephone conversations over-heard, even by the most sympathetic listener. Perhaps I knew, subconsciously, whom the call would be from, but I refused to admit it to myself.

Beginning to fidget, I asked for a dry martini, and when its soothing influence had worn off, for another. Why did I feel so rattled? I was not bankrupt, I was not being blackmailed, I had no urgent financial problems. I could not think of any reason why somebody in London should ring me up—and ring me up twice, for the call must be expensive.

But the prospect of it got on my nerves, and I had almost

decided to say I was not available when the man came in and said: 'The telephone call for you, signore.'

The telephone call, as if there was only one! I followed him to the instrument.

'Pronto!'

'Pronto!'

'Pronto!'

'Pronto!'

The usual exchange of prontos.

'Pronto, chi parla?' I said in some exasperation.

'Pronto, chi parla?' echoed the operator.

It turned out to be Barbara, and just as her voice and her name were uniting to make the Barbara I knew, Myra crossed the room and gave me a quick look.

'Yes, Barbara.'

A horrible crackling ensued.

'Can you hear me, Edward?'

'Yes, but very faintly.'

'It's about Gilbert.'

Some words followed which I couldn't catch. Perhaps my self-defence mechanism didn't want me to catch them.

'You say he's—'

A sentence followed that had the sound of sense without the meaning. Barbara repeated it, dwelling on each word.

'He wants to come here?' I repeated. 'Gilbert wants to come here? But why?'

In Barbara's reply the one word I could really understand was 'Myra' and I looked round hastily, but she wasn't to be seen. The crackling continued.

'I wish that they could clear the line. What has *she*'—I wouldn't mention her name—'to do with it?'

Barbara's answer came through clearly enough, too clearly.

'He wants to see her.'

'Well, he will see her when she gets back. She isn't'—I glanced round—'going to be here much longer.'

'But he wants to see her *now*. He wants to *give* her something.'

'But this is stupid, Barbara,' I said with rising irritation. 'Surely he can wait a day or two.'

'No, he wants to see her now.'

'But why?'

'Because he isn't well, he isn't at all well, Edward.'

'Do you want me to tell her that?'

'Yes, please. Be a good boy, please, Edward. He says that if she doesn't come to England, he'll go to Assisi.'

'Well, let him.'

'But, he's not fit to travel. Really he isn't. If he comes, I shall come with him. He really isn't fit to travel alone.'

'What's the matter with him?' At this point Myra passed through the room again, with a questioning look at me; and at the same moment the telephone, having made noises of outraged impatience, gave out and was silent. I held on to it for what seemed minutes, but it was dead, completely dead.

'You were having a long talk,' said Myra, coming up to me. 'I hope it was a pleasant one.'

'Not altogether.'

'May I know what it was about, or were you talking secrets?'

I realized that the terms Myra and I were now on, gave her a perfect right to ask such a question.

'No, of course, I have no secrets from you . . . But . . .'

'But you don't want to tell me just now?' Myra said.

'Well, give me a little time to sort my thoughts out.'

'Yes, indeed,' said Myra. 'And don't tell me anything if you'd rather not.'

*

I spent a miserable afternoon threshing about with my thoughts. What would happen if I told Myra what Barbara had said? She was bound to be upset, but would she be upset for me, so to speak, or against me? My fears had far less difficulty than my hopes in answering that question. By representations and persuasions I had won Myra over from her attachment to Gilbert: I had convinced her mind, no doubt; I had led her to see that at our age, and in our circumstances, we could look forward to a happier life together than either of us could apart, certainly happier than Myra could, dancing attendance on Gilbert, following Cupid for his loaves and fishes. He was innately selfish, of that I was sure. But had I convinced her heart? Her heart didn't mind his selfishness, had even thrived on it, these many years. Her heart would respond to the lightest call, the faintest throb, from his: the knowledge that he still needed her, that he was ill because of her absence and that in spite of illness he wanted to travel out and see her—these emotional considerations would outweigh any of my carefully thought-out arguments, my affection, which she must have believed in, or even my love, which she may have believed in, but only as one believes in the power of an ace to take a trick.

My fears persuaded me that the smallest hint of the purpose of Barbara's telephone-call would upset the balance of Myra's feelings, so precariously dipping in my favour.

And what had my hopes to offer? Only that she, a clever, talented attractive woman, admired by many and loved perhaps by some, would see the folly of her ways and forgo the shadow for the substance. She might, she might—for Myra was not a fool.

But even if she did, what would be her reaction on discovering, as discover she might, sooner or later, that I had deceived her by withholding one vital piece of information? We might be safely married by that time—by the time that Gilbert, or Barbara, or someone else put her wise—but would she forgive me? No, she would hate me, and our marriage would last no longer, in reality if not in fact, than the words of abiding loyalty that we uttered in church, for of course we should be married in church— Myra was church-going to some extent, and so was I, and there was nothing in our past lives—certainly nothing in mine—to deter us from a religious ceremony.

Chapter Eighteen

WE DINED on the terrace of the hotel, that overlooks the plain of Perugia. Gradually, on the far side, to the west under the hills, the familiar line of greenish lights appeared: they might have marked a town, but as far as I knew there was no town, so it could have been a road. In the sky, descending from the sky and rising from the ground, was a bluish-grey light, twilight, I suppose, but like no twilight I had ever seen in Assisi or elsewhere. I kept turning to look at it from the dining-room where there was a flashing fountain, dolphins, and other marine creatures, motionlessly disporting themselves for the tourists' delight.

'You're very silent,' said Myra. 'I hope that nothing is worrying you.'

'Oh no,' I said, 'how could it?' and I turned again to the blue-grey evening, which darkness would soon engulf.

'All the same, I think there is something on your mind,' said Myra. 'You've been different, somehow, since you had that telephone-call. I don't want to pry, Edward, and I'm sure it has nothing to do with me, but if it has, or even if it hasn't, please tell me. I don't want only to share your happy times, and you have given me so many. Gilbert'—she stopped.

'Yes, Myra?'

'There has been so much more sunshine than cloud, if you see what I mean, and now that I'm acclimatized to the difference—'

'Yes?'

'I don't want to go back, I've turned the corner. So I felt anxious for myself, as well as for you, when I saw you struggling with the telephone.'

'Oh, the Italian telephone,' I said, 'it is so exasperating. You can only hear one word in five. The Italians are wonderful engineers and yet—'

'But one happy-sounding word makes all the rest sound happy, doesn't it, even if one doesn't hear them properly? That was why—'

'You thought I wasn't hearing that happy-sounding word.'

'Frankly, yes. You looked worried and anxious. I don't like to see you look like that.'

'Listen, Myra,' I said. 'You are right: it wasn't very good news. The call was from Barbara, she says she thinks of coming to Assisi.'

'Barbara? but why?'

'I couldn't understand why, the line was so terribly noisy. And when she was coming to the point, so to speak, we were cut off.'

'Barbara? Barbara?' Myra repeated, and her face showed as much anxiety as mine must have had at the telephone. 'Why should *she* want to come?'

'She has a perfect right to come, of course,' I answered. 'Italy is a free country, freer, in some ways than England. But I think it was a little tactless of her.'

'You mean because she knew that you and I—'

'We didn't make a secret of it, did we? I was going to Assisi to paint, you were coming for . . . for a holiday. I left my address with my factotum, as I expect you left yours with your dear Mrs. Frensham. Barbara could have got it from either of them— but I forgot that I wrote to her, which was how she knew my telephone number.'

'Do you think Barbara is in love with you?' asked Myra. 'I had always thought that if she was in love with anyone, it was Gilbert.'

'I think you're right,' I said. 'I'm sure that if she had been in love with me, I should have known it. People don't make that sort of mistake, do they?'

'Well, sometimes they do, Edward, sometimes they do. What a pity she didn't explain why she was coming. We belong to our age and are not shockable but all the same, I do think it was odd she didn't show more—more consideration. "Two's company" is a proverb older even than we are. Barbara is quite civilized—she must have some reason, that seems to her a good reason—for wanting to make a third. I can only suppose she is in love with you. I wish I knew what she was after. Couldn't you ring her up?'

'It wouldn't be any good, Myra,' I said, wearily, warily. 'There would be the same chorus of prontos, and crackles, and explosions, and we shouldn't get any forrader.'

'Did she say when she was coming?'

'No, I gathered it might be fairly soon.'

Myra began to show agitation. I knew the signs; her lips trembled and her voice was not quite under control when she said: 'Then what *are* we to do?'

At that moment a flash of sheet lightning lit up the plain of Perugia, almost extinguishing the line of greenish lights under the hills opposite, but bringing into vivid prominence the great church of Santa Maria degli Angeli, a mile or so away. Unknown to us, a thunderstorm had been brewing up on the hills behind Assisi, and this was the first manifestation of it—a manifestation that was not at all blinding, but in its black and white definition of the whole crowded but not complex landscape, marvellously illuminating; and the same light, so positive and so un-mysterious, seemed to flash upon my mind, too.

'There are two things we can do,' I said. 'The first is just practical, but none the less useful. We can leave Assisi, and go to some other place.'

'But what about your pictures?'

'I've finished them, except the second one of the Rocca, and that will only take a day or two.'

'And then where shall we go?'

'To Spoleto, don't you think? There's quite a good hotel, and the Festival is just beginning—its the most natural thing in the world for us to move there, and we needn't even bother to leave our address. I'll ring up the hotel tomorrow. Spoleto is a lovely place, quite as beautiful as Assisi, really, and just as paintable, if not as holy.'

Myra considered this, and the cloud left her brow.

'Yes, I think it would be a good idea. Barbara could hardly follow us to Spoleto, could she?' and she gave a laugh that was almost a giggle. 'Forgive me,' she said, coughing, 'but I still feel she has designs on you . . . and I don't mean to give you up to her—oh, no, Edward, I don't.'

Those words were sweet to hear.

'But you said there was something else that we could do,' she said suddenly. 'I can't imagine being happier than I am now, but perhaps I could be. You are such a good purveyor of happiness.'

She smiled at me across the table but all at once the smile changed to a look of alarm as if she had been thunder-struck—and no wonder, for the clap of thunder overhead made the cutlery and glass rattle on the table.

Surprised out of ourselves, we blinked, as though to keep the phenomenal world at bay; a moment later we blinked again, as though to welcome it back.

She wasn't ashamed of showing fright, and the reaction to confidence and safety was all the stronger.

'What was it you were saying?' she asked, her nerves still shaken, but her old self, the self I loved, coming through her nervousness. 'You said there was something else we might do, besides eloping to Spoleto.'

I got up from the table and came towards her.

'Need you ask?' I said, 'stay here,' and none of the other diners noticed our embrace, they are so used to such things in Italy, and so pleased by them, and by what is the natural outcome of them.

Chapter Nineteen

IN TOKEN of our new intimacy we engaged a double-bedded room in the hotel at Spoleto: Myra wanted this as much as I did. But the room was not available for three days, and as our hotel at Assisi was full up we had to content ourselves, formally at any rate, with single strictness.

Those were happy days, those first days of our complete, uninterrupted communion. I didn't feel that we needed to make 'plans', for all plans were so subordinate to the execution of our one plan, that individually, as separate problems, separate stumbling-blocks, they hardly existed. If we didn't always walk about hand in hand, like younger lovers, we sometimes did, and I think the functionaries at the hotel were pleased with our mutual solicitude, so solicitous were they for us, such smiles of sympathy did they bestow upon us, when we came in, or went out together.

Together-ness—how well the Latins understand it.

I was finishing my second picture of the Rocca, in which I managed to include,—to my satisfaction, at any rate,—the many sided tower with its hexagonal lantern (a faint suggestion of the central tower of Ely Cathedral) built perhaps a century before Pope Pius II added his final addition to the castle, more decorative, I imagined, than defensive. To get it in, and include the Keep, by far the most imposing feature of the building, I had to foreshorten the wall which linked them, and which, by its immense length and height and the multitude of colours composing it, had always fascinated me. I tried various ways of suggesting its pictorial importance,—its strategic importance was quite obvious. I took my stand, or my seat, at the furthest possible limit of the hill, where the ground falls away, almost in precipices, on three sides. Three ways to fall! And on one side, far below, was appropriately enough the cemetery, a level oblong on a foothill, with its tombstones and its chapel, girt by funereal cypresses and topiary yews. And all kept so beautifully in order, not a headstone, not a stone even, looked neglected. Death kept up to date.

To get to my pitch I had to carry my painting materials from the car-park along the ragged, outward curving footpath that skirted the summit of the hill. Brambles and honeysuckle, and travellers' joy, acacias and olive trees fenced it on the left, otherwise the drop would have been too steep for my comfort, for I have a bad head for heights.

But once precariously perched on my stool, whether or not Myra was with me, I forgot the dizzy depth below, into which an unguarded flourish with my paint-brush, or a backward tilt of disgust, might easily have plunged me.

In front of and between me and the castle-wall was a long stretch of what might have been called turf—it was short enough, but, bleached by the rigour of the Italian sun, it was scarcely darker than hay. Level as a meadow, it stretched to a bunch of hillocks and hollows beneath the castle walls, grass-grown survivals of some former outwork of defence.

Here I would sit, completely absorbed in trying to find a satisfactory relationship between the dusty pink of the walls, and the tufts of yellowing grass below them—colours which Nature had subtly accommodated to each other,—until Myra came. She was the climax of the experience, and she bore me away, and some of my painting gear too, for she insisted on carrying it to the taxi waiting at the car-park. Much as I resented the car-park in that time-mellowed twice-hallowed setting from which the centuries had withdrawn the threat of violence, leaving only the harmless majesty of antiquity, I was grateful for it.

So passed the first three mornings, in what I can only call the most blissful of all unions, the mutual union of art and love, which many have enjoyed before, but I, never until now.

She knew my dislike of heights, and would walk between me

and the declivity, but even so I often kept my eyes on the parched rock-earth of the pathway, in which the active and pervasive ants had drilled tiny craters, miniature volcanoes, that seemed deeper for the ring of powdered earth they had thrown up round them. 'For God's sake let us sit upon the ground,' said Richard II; I shouldn't have dared to; but I sometimes suspected that these ubiquitous little creatures clung to the feathery outwork of oats (such a frail defence against armed attack) that bordered the pathway on the Castle side. Scenting my arrival, they somehow leapt across, and did me more bodily harm than the Guelf or the Ghibelline troops, whichever happened to be in possession of the stronghold, pouring boiling oil through its huge machicolations, ever could have. Oats, bleached white, and barley, honey-coloured, and deep blue borage, with humming bird hawk-moths darting between them, fringed one side—the safe side—of the way round the Castle.

It was our last and happiest day in Assisi, we were going on to Spoleto the next morning; lunch awaited us and a blissful siesta afterwards. My regret at leaving Assisi only touched the surface of my mind, so deeply was it imbued with happy thoughts, with a sense of fulfilment as indivisible as a cardinal number. So that when the page-boy, the *piccolo*, came up to me with a flimsy crumpled envelope in his hand, I thought he had mistaken me for someone else. But he left me in no doubt.

'Per lei, signore,' he said impressively, 'for *you*.' I saw my name on it, and correctly spelt, too.

Myra had gone away to powder her nose; I was glad I was alone. 'Very worried,' I read, 'Gilbert gone away suddenly leaving no address stop—is he with you?'

The telegram was signed Barbara, and contained a slip of paper pre-paying a reply.

The page-boy was still standing beside me: it took me a few moments to collect my thoughts. The telegram had been sent at nine o'clock that morning.

I wrote hastily, 'Gilbert not here,' and something made me add, 'Am leaving for Spoleto, tomorrow.' I gave the boy the paper and a tip and he marched off with an important air. On an impulse I followed him out of the room and made for the receptionist's desk. He was engaged with other matters, as they so often are; but presently he turned to me and asked me, more or less politely, what I wanted.

'Has a Mr. Gilbert Finstock engaged a room at the hotel?'

The concierge consulted his ledger.

'No, signore.'

Much relieved, but not entirely reassured, I went to the bar, which like the lounge was decorated with a mural of over-loaded grape-vines, with youths and maidens sporting in their shade. I felt that even good news can be made better by a stiff dry Martini or two. Here I was joined by Myra, looking as radiant as she had all through the past few days. All she needed was tomato juice,— to quench her thirst, not to settle her spirits. With a woman's intuition she noticed the cloud on mine, and said:

'Has the post come yet?'

Postal deliveries at Assisi were very irregular; and it suddenly struck me that if the letters hadn't come, they might come at any moment.

'Excuse me,' I said, though it seemed a rather formal way of addressing Myra, who was by now used to my excuses, 'but I'll go and ask at the desk.'

Yes, the mail had arrived, but there was nothing for me.

'Nor anything for the Signora?'

I forgot that Myra would be registered as Miss.

'No signore.'

'Nor anything for Signor Gilbert Finstock?'

The man rather irritably replied 'No!' His annoyance calmed me more than a civil reply would have.

'Were you expecting another letter from Barbara?' asked Myra, when I told her that my errand had been fruitless.

'No . . . Why do you ask?'

'I just thought she might have written again.'

'Oh, she doesn't write to me often, we were never on those terms,' I said.

With this Myra seemed satisfied; we lunched almost in the old carefree manner; and when we retired for our siestas I found to my surprise that I could sleep.

Painting in the afternoon was different of course from in the morning; the sun had gone round, and striking the castle walls, not only altered the shadows but seemed to bleach the stone-work. The picture was nearly finished, and there were many things in it I didn't want to touch; but there were mistakes of drawing which could be corrected without much reference to the change of light.

I worked hard at these, and at about six o'clock, when the sun's level rays were losing their fierceness, I was putting on the finishing touches. Between the almost automatic process of looking up and looking down, my eye caught sight of a figure coming along the pathway. It was Myra, lit up from head to foot, and more completely visible than I had ever seen her.

She put her camp-stool beside mine, and sat down without our usual precautions against falling over backwards.

'I've come a bit earlier than usual,' she said, rather breath-lessly, 'because a telegram came for you, which I thought you would want to see.'

She took it from her bag and handed it to me, saying, 'I'll just take a look from the furthest point at the view over the cemetery and across to the hills. I love it, and we may not see it again.'

With that she rose, rather abruptly, and the accident I had always dreaded happened: her stool toppled over, and I was only just in time to put out my arm and save her from going with it. In the effort to do this I knocked over my painting apparatus, which went one way while my paint-box went another: it was all a flurry and a scramble, and it took us a moment or two to convince ourselves that no real harm had been done.

Myra's camp-stool was soon retrieved from the bushes below; and my painting-gear, which hadn't gone downhill, needed no retrieving.

'That was lucky!' I said, panting. 'You're not hurt are you, darling? But you must be frightened. Painting has many drawbacks, but I never thought of it as dangerous to life and limb!'

She smiled at me, smoothing down her dress and putting her hat straight—she always wore one, for she hated getting sunburnt. Then, having restored her appearance and given herself a little shake, she said:

'But I can't find the telegram. Is it lost? It can't be!'

I couldn't remember what happened at the moment of Myra's upset. We hunted high and low, especially low, as far as we dared go; but the brambles and the honeysuckle, if they held the secret, kept it to themselves.

After several minutes of frustrated search, in which we both sustained severe scratches from the brambles, we turned to each other in despair.

Myra tried to console me. 'I don't suppose it was really important! Just . . . just . . . a telegram.'

'Let's have one last look,' I said.

But like many last looks, this one was no more rewarding than its predecessors. Turning our backs on the brambles we searched for the telegram on the sun-scorched plateau below the Castle; but though Italian tourists leave little litter, we couldn't detect a buff-coloured slip of paper where Nature itself was buff-coloured.

'If only I had left it at the hotel,' sighed Myra. 'That comes of being a busybody.'

'Or if you had read it,' said I, disingenuously.

'Oh, I couldn't have done that!'

'You're sure it was for me?'

'Yes, yes, now go on with your painting, and I will contemplate the cemetery.'

She left me, walking slowly. She had a loose long-limbed stride, almost a lurch. Should I put her into the picture? She would fit nicely there, at the foot of the terminal tower. Just a suggestion of her bending forwards, peering down into the gulf, where lay the cemetery, which for some reason appealed to both of us, and beyond it, the valley enclosed by steep hills bright with yellow broom where they were not dark with the foliage of the trees in summer.

Her figure would give a better impression of the height of the tower than did the tourists, clinging fly-like to its top-most railing. I made some rapid strokes; there she was, or someone like her, a little bowed, as befitted a visitor to Assisi, making obeisance to that holy place. I turned towards her, thinking she might look back at me, as people sometimes do look back, as though responding to an unheard call; but she didn't, and my returning gaze caught a gleam of yellow, which might have been a shred of toilet-paper, impaled and fluttering like a flag on one of the brambles at my back. I measured the distance and the danger; I half made up my mind to have a go; and then a passing breeze wafted the object, whatever it was, out of sight.

Myra was coming back, over the parched grass, which looked dead but wasn't, shading her eyes from the declining sun. I began to pack my traps, but first I wanted to show her what I had done.

'There you are!' I said, pointing to the figure by the tower. 'I mean, there *you* are. It wouldn't have been complete without you!'

'You've made me look very small,' she said, and kissed me. 'But there is something that rather worries me,' she added, 'the telegram. Do you think it can have been important? Ought we to ask the post-office to have it repeated?'

'I doubt if they would,' I said, gathering up the utensils of my trade, 'and besides, the post-office must be shut by now. Don't let's bother about it, Myra—we almost risked our lives to recover it. It disappeared by an act of God.'

As women so often do, she looked only half-satisfied.

'We shall know in the end,' I said, as soothingly as I could.

*

Our taxi was waiting for us. How short the way down, compared to the laborious ascent. I never changed for dinner, but Myra always made alterations to her dress and to her appearance.

Large or small, they always took her some time, and, as before, I beguiled her absence with a visit to the concierge's desk. It had become a routine procedure. I hardly knew why I went, or what I expected to hear, for now, at this last hour of our sojourn in Assisi, our *viaggio di nozze*, our unofficial honeymoon, you might call it, there was no reason to go because there was nothing to hear. Nonetheless, I went, as I had done before.

'Niente per me?' I asked, and then in case he didn't understand my Italian, 'nothing for me?'

'There was a telegram for the signore,' he said, meaning me, not God, for whom the word is sometimes used; 'but the signora took it to give to you.'

'Ah, yes,' I said.

'But another telegram came later,' he continued, 'not for you, signore, but for *us*. *Per noi*,'—and with an expansive gesture he seemed to embrace all the hotel. 'It was from an English person. Perhaps a friend of yours?'

He brought out a folded form and handed it to me.

'E un nome difficile,' he said. 'N . . N . . '

'Newhouse,' I finished it for him. 'Yes, it is a difficult name'—and none the less difficult, I thought, for being Barbara's. 'Yes, I do know her. I see she wants a room for three days. Can you give her one?'

'Sissignore. It happens that we can. We shall have a room to spare since you and the signora are going away tomorrow.'

'Yes,' I said, 'in the morning.'

'What a pity,' said the concierge, with the ready sympathy of Italians for one's personal affairs. 'But perhaps you and your friend will meet here or at Spoleto. Spoleto is not very distant.'

'Perhaps we shall,' I said, and went to join Myra in the vine-clad bar.

Chapter Twenty

'YOU seem a little distrait,' said Myra who had accomplished that subtle transformation that women so easily achieve, unlike men, who, unless they suddenly grow beards or moustaches, or both, look more or less the same, except in so far as age has changed them—'I hope that nothing has gone wrong?'

'Oh no,' I said, and then it occurred to me that unless we succeeded in avoiding Barbara, many things might go wrong. Myra was bound to find out, sooner or later, that Barbara was or had been in Assisi, and she would never trust me again.

'The concierge told me that Barbara had booked a room here.'

Myra's eyes, and the sudden tilt of her head, showed how startled she was.

'Barbara? But why on earth—'

'Well, we are on earth,' I said, trying to smile.

'Yes, of course, but why, and when is she coming?'

'My darling, I can only tell you what the concierge told me, that a certain Signora Newhouse had taken a room here for tomorrow.'

'By which time *we* shall be gone?'

Myra tried to hide her agitation.

'Of course, dearest,' I said. 'We're going soon after breakfast.' I looked at my watch. 'It's nearly nine o'clock now.'

'You don't think we could go *tonight*?' said Myra.

'We could try,' I said, anxious to fall in with her wishes, or her whims. 'But the Festival at Spoleto is on, and I doubt if the rooms,—the room—would be available. Anyhow, what have we to fear from Barbara? She's a friend of both of us.'

'Oh nothing, nothing,' Myra said. 'It's different for a woman, perhaps you wouldn't understand, but I don't like the idea of meeting Barbara. Should we go for a walk, darling, a gentle stroll till bedtime? It's so good for the digestion.'

Before I could agree or disagree she had risen to her feet.

I followed her from the dining-room. We took the lift up to the ground floor, went to the hotel door, and looked out into the street.

'Which way now?' I asked.

'Oh, does it matter?'

'Let's go towards San Francesco,' I said, pointing to the left. 'I think I could stagger that far. And then if you feel energetic enough, Myra, we could go on upwards, excelsior, excelsior, until we get to the newspaper-shop in the Piazza and that rather disagreeable round-faced woman. I know how much you rely on getting yesterday's *Times*—much more than on getting *our* news,' I added, trying to tease her, and quite certain that she wouldn't agree to this post-prandial prance.

'But won't the shop be shut?' she asked.

'It mightn't be. Italian shops are not like ours, they keep open at all hours.'

She saw the joke, such as it was, and laughed. She never lacked a sense of humour or rather, a tolerance of my sense of humour.

'But aren't all hours our hours?' she said, at which we both laughed.

By now we were struggling up the long, steep hill to the Piazza.

'Should we stop at the Oratorio dei Pellegrini, the Chapel of Perpetual Adoration?' she asked suddenly. 'I like it so much. It's always open day and night, longer than the shops, it has to be. I suppose the nuns take it in turns, there must be a time-limit even for prayer,—especially, perhaps, for prayer.'

'Just as you please,' I said, surprised at her request, for I hadn't realized she was religious. 'But let's pop in on our way back. The newspaper shop may not be open, but, as you say, the chapel always is.'

Under the strain of hill-climbing, after a substantial meal, our conversation languished. But once we had passed the splendid

Roman pillars of the church, now Christian, once dedicated to Minerva, and the gay little café where sometimes we stopped off, on the way up, for our elevenses, we found the newspaper-shop, to my astonishment, still open.

'Il Times di Londra, per piacere?' I asked unhopefully of that grim-faced, round-faced woman.

Without a word she handed it to me.

'Trovato!' I exclaimed to Myra, emerging with the newspaper in my hand. 'Now you'll be happy for at least an hour.'

'Thank you,' she said, and began peering at it. 'But I can't read it, you know. In spite of all the lights, it's much too dark.'

'Keep it till we get back,' I said, 'then you can read it at your leisure. Let me carry it for you.'

Still slightly out of breath, we started on the downward journey.

'Oh, the *chapel*!' Myra cried. 'Where is it? Have we passed it?'

Even by day the entrance to the chapel wasn't easy to find: its round topped doorway lurked in the street wall, as did so many other round-topped doorways. Eventually we found it and went in.

It was a small place, hardly bigger than a good-sized room. One light burned in the central chandelier, and twelve candles on the altar, where the Sacrament was already exposed. Coming from the sun-deserted street, the dim religious light enabled us to see a little. I say 'us', because by now I assumed that Myra and I shared the same thoughts and impressions, the same liberties and limitations. The frescoes were early works of the Lorenzetti period. They covered the ceiling and the walls. Dimly discerned, they made the chapel seem still smaller than it was. An aisle divided the two rows of pews. In the front row on the left, facing the altar, knelt the two nuns whose turn it was to keep the unbroken vigil of the chapel.

Except for the two nuns, we had the chapel to ourselves. I think we instinctively felt that our orisons would not be as acceptable as theirs, so we sat at the back and tried to make ourselves invisible, which wasn't difficult. I am not very religious but such religion as I have found its readiest outlet in this chapel.

Perpetual Adoration! Perpetual Adoration! But of what, and why? I didn't have to ask myself these questions, nor I think, did Myra, who I knew frequented the chapel on her sight-seeing jaunts—it was only ten minutes' walk from our hotel.

Perpetual Adoration excluded the sense of sin, thank goodness; all one had to do was to adore, as the two nuns, perhaps two Poor Clares, were doing. No doubt they had a better idea of what adoration meant than we had—we were unworthy to pick up the scraps from the table of adoration. But still we,— I keep saying we—now that I was plural—felt that in spite of ourselves, in spite of the state of the world, there was someone or something to adore.

I remembered Smart's poem, where the meaning of adoration is conveyed with incomparable eloquence, and I bent my head in my hands, and moved a little way away from Myra, for fear she should be aware of and embarrassed by my emotion, the obligation to adore. Not each other, for I could not suppose that the Chapel of Perpetual Adoration took cognisance of human love—but the Power that had, in spite of everything that was opposed in our temperaments and our circumstances and, it might be added in our consciences, brought us together. No power within ourselves, I was now convinced, could have done it; so how could we not adore the Power that did?

Overcome by gratitude, I was aware of the divine dispensation almost as if it was a physical blessing that had been accorded me, the miraculous recovery from an illness, a bullet that had just missed me, a head-on collision with an approaching car that had somehow been averted. Thinking of how amazingly fortunate I was, how extraordinarily favoured, I quite forgot the self I had brought into the chapel, and was aware only of beams of celestial brightness that seemed to pass round me and over me, and through me—of which I was the object but to which, thanks to the grace given me, I was also able to respond, and to give out, in my feeble way, feelings not altogether different in kind from those I was receiving, feelings of adoration, of perpetual adoration, for they were timeless.

135

How long I knelt I do not know. It was a feeling that I had someone to consider besides myself, and that Myra might not be so lost in adoration as I was, that made me look up and steal a glance at her, across the space between. She, too, seemed utterly absorbed in her private thoughts and I think it was telepathy, not any direct form of communication, that made her lift her head, for she looked at me as if I had been a stranger.

'Edward dear,' she murmured, 'perhaps—' I knew what she meant: perhaps, we ought to go. I had no idea what time it was, but the hotel, for all its merits, did not keep late hours. But I did not want to go, nor, I think, did she: the magic of the place still held us, and was irrecoverable outside. As if possessed by a single impulse, we each again fell on our knees hid our faces. But it was no good, the spell was broken.

I was the first to give up trying, and lifted my face into the gloom. Myra's was still hidden by her hands, though I could see her lips moving. I stretched my stiff limbs, unaccustomed to perpetual, or even occasional adoration, and tried to imprint on my memory the shape and feeling of the chapel,—perhaps I would one day try to paint it, in all its shades of darkness. The two Poor Clares (if such they were) were still kneeling, heedless of the temporal, engrossed by the eternal; but there was another figure, sitting half-right from us, and much nearer to the altar, who certainly hadn't been there when we came. It wasn't strange —his presence wasn't strange, any more than ours was, perhaps less strange, if he was a Roman Catholic, for whom the benefits of the chapel were intended, whereas we were outsiders, having no right to them. Nor was it strange that he should have come in without my noticing him, without *our* noticing him, for I felt sure that Myra hadn't either. I would ask her later, when she had emerged from her devotions. Meanwhile for lack of anything else to do, I studied the man's back, bowed in worship as the nuns were. Like theirs it was black, a deeper shade of darkness in the general gloom, and something about it seemed to be familiar. Yet how could anyone's back, in such murky conditions, be familiar? Then he turned his head towards the altar, and its extraordinary pallor, as of parchment, lit by a candle from within, made me recognize him at once.

I leaned across the aisle to Myra: she started at my touch. I made some gesture—I don't know what—and she nodded and picked up her bag. In a few moments we were out in the street.

The street was as dark as the chapel had been; it was straight for an Assisi street, but like the other streets it was narrow, and we sometimes had to clutch each other to avoid being run over. The moon hadn't risen, and the gleams left over from the departed sunset did not fall on the façade of the church of San Francesco, which, owing to the lie of the land, had to face east, not west. It hid its face from us. We should not see it again, but from such hints and reminders as the darkness gave I tried to remember what it looked like, and how it differed from those other churches that looked down on it across the town, San Rufino and Santa Chiara.

The road broadened as it turned leftwards through the colonnades beyond which lay our hotel.

It was bedtime, but I had never felt less like going to bed. A nightcap had never been a habit with me, but I thought for once I would have one, and perhaps induce Myra to have one as well. She hadn't seen what I had seen, but she would see it,—sooner or later, if not tonight.

There were several possible explanations. My mind, fluttering round the problem like a bee too tired to make its way back to the hive, tried to decide which was the most likely. The true solution no doubt lay in Barbara's telegram, which I should never see, though it might still be in existence, caught in a thicket on the hill below the Rocca, but probably by now torn into shreds. What *could* she have said, except that she was coming to Assisi, a fact that I had confirmed at the receptionist's desk? But *why* was she coming? Not to embarrass me and Myra—it was quite unlike Barbara to do that. She was too civilized, and besides she liked us both, however much she disapproved of us. Had she said that Gilbert was coming with her? That might be it, for she had told me that he was too unwell to travel alone. He *might* have come with her and put up somewhere else. In Assisi there were plenty of hotels, the San Francesco hotel, the Cimabue hotel, the Giotto hotel, advertisements proclaiming them littered the roadside. Or had they put their heads together and booked a room for Barbara which really was for Gilbert? Such a plan would appeal to Gilbert's ingenious sense of humour (which the critics had noticed in his music) and he might have persuaded Barbara to fall in with it, and it would be in keeping with the remark he had made to her about being 'a shadowy third' to keep us company. I didn't believe that he was too ill to travel by himself. He often complained of feeling ill, and his nerves were disordered, as appeared often—too often—in his music.

But the fact remained that he was here in Assisi—I had seen him although Myra hadn't—and we should have to do something about it. I didn't think he would turn up in our midst; there was no room for him at the hotel, or for Barbara, if she was representing him—until tomorrow, when Myra and I were due to vacate our rooms.

I remembered that Myra would have liked to go away tonight. We must leave tomorrow at crack of dawn, and if our room at the Hotel dei Principi at Spoleto wasn't ready for us, we would while away the time in sight-seeing.

The bar was closed, but a waiter, still rather blearily on duty, said he would bring me a whisky and soda. It arrived at the same time that Myra did, and I persuaded her to have one with me. I had decided not to tell her that I had seen Gilbert in the chapel of Perpetual Adoration—it would only upset her, as it had upset me, and do no good. From the vantage point of Spoleto, our strategic position would be much stronger. Perhaps it was a mistake to have told Barbara that I (did I say I?) was going there, but we could easily go somewhere else, if . . . if . . .

Chapter Twenty-one

MYRA seemed to have quite recovered from the little panic or whatever it was, that had disturbed her after dinner. She apologized for it. 'I can't think what came over me,' she said. 'I'm not usually so silly, but sometimes I had a sort of spiritual shudder, I suppose rather like people have when they say that someone is walking over their grave! I feel much, *much* better now, dear Edward, though still not quite like *myself*—don't laugh—I'm not so very keen on being like myself! But one's friends do expect it of one, don't they? Especially one's *men* friends—not you, Edward, you are in a class apart. I mean, a sort of consistency of feeling, and behaviour that comes more easily to men than women. Much as I loved dear Gilbert, and still do, I confess I got exasperated by him sometimes. Not because he expected me to be always at his beck and call, I quite liked that, then, and his dependence on me, though I shouldn't like it now—but because whatever mood *he* was in, and you know how cantankerous he could be, especially when his work was worrying him, he expected *me* to be always calm and collected, he was so *selfish,* but then men *are* selfish, with certain honourable exceptions.'

Remembering the many hours that Myra had spent sitting beside me on a camp-stool, discouraged even from looking at what I was doing, for I hated to be overlooked while I was painting, I listened to this tirade in shame and silence.

'But he's a dear fellow, really,' Myra went on, 'perhaps the most worthwhile person we have known—no comparisons meant, for your art, your intention, are so utterly different from his, if he has an intention. Why am I talking like this?' she interrupted herself. 'I don't generally, do I, Edward? And I'm not drunk,' she said, eyeing her untouched glass. 'You must have a bad effect on me, and in future I shall be known as Myra the Messalina. But shall I tell you what has really unloosened my tongue, and made me so indiscreet? It was those minutes, hours, days, I don't know how long—that we spent in the chapel—they must have had a *liberating* effect on me. Perpetual adoration! You see it includes everything, things that are adorable, and things that aren't! Don't be alarmed Edward; I shall come to myself in a moment or two and be as inarticulate and submissive, and above all, as *appreciative,* as Gilbert could have wished.'

She gave me a mischievous smile, that didn't seem to belong to her pre-chapel days; and then with a sudden change of mood she said, 'What's that you have under your arm? Is it the newspaper?'

I was as surprised as she was; to think I had been clutching it to me all this time!

'We went out to get it,' I reminded her. 'It was our *but de promenade,* so to speak.'

'And you kept it from me all this time?'

'You didn't ask for it,' I said, 'it wasn't part of our religious observances, and you were so busy talking. I haven't seen it, either. But here it is.'

I handed her the newspaper, and she unfolded it.

'I don't know that I want to read it now,' she said, almost pettishly. 'It's a day old, isn't it, and there's nothing in it perpetual or adorable, is there? Only what is ephemeral and well . . . unadorable. What shall I look at first?'

'I generally look at the letters, and then the front page, and then the Home News, and then the financial columns—'

'Oh, how different you are from me,' Myra exclaimed. ' "Unlike, unlike are we, oh princely heart!" My interests are more personal. I look first at the births, marriages and deaths.'

She found the column where they were, her eyes ran down it, and suddenly her face went quite pale.

'Here,' she said, with her finger on the entry. 'Please help me, Edward, please, please help me.'

Her left arm dropped to her side and the newspaper slid to the floor. She looked at it in a daze, and picked it up, and clung to it. I thought she was going to faint. I held the whisky to her lips— it was all I could think of—and she swallowed a little of it, and coughed.

'But who would have *believed* it!' she kept repeating. 'Who would have *believed it*?'

'Believed what, Myra darling? What is it that has upset you so much?'

But she didn't, or couldn't, or wouldn't tell me.

I helped her upstairs to her room, and fed her with sleeping pills and tranquillizers. She didn't want me to stay, she didn't want me to go, and I had been in and out half a dozen times before she fell asleep.

The *Times* was lying by her bedside on the floor, where she had dropped it.

I tiptoed out and took it to my room, for the light in the passage was too dim to read by.

I am slow at finding paragraphs in newspapers, but I thought I knew where this one would be, and turned at once to the Deaths. But Gilbert's name wasn't there, as indeed how could it be, when I had seen him scarcely an hour ago in the chapel? I turned the pages until I came to the obituary column. Even if his relations had omitted to put his name among the deaths, surely I should find some reference to him there, for though not much esteemed as a composer by the general public, he was highly regarded by some critics. No, nothing.

Then I began to wonder if I was mistaken in thinking that Myra's distress had anything to do with Gilbert. She had many friends, of course, some of whose names I knew: it might only be my uneasy conscience that attributed her grief to Gilbert. So I scanned the two sad columns again, but could not find a name that tolled the faintest bell. Where, then, where had Myra's eye, so much keener than mine, discovered these disastrous tidings? And yes, there it was, a tiny paragraph in a bottom left-hand corner. 'Mr. Gilbert Finstock, the well-known composer, has disappeared from his flat in Roland Gardens, leaving no address. The police are carrying out investigations, but there is no suspicion of foul play.'

So perhaps it was all a mare's nest on which Myra, whose conscience was as uneasy as mine, had put a sinister construction.

It was nearly midnight, but I decided that I should rest more comfortably if I made the only inquiry that was left open to me. I told the night-porter that I was going out for half an hour or so, at which he gave me a rather sleepy smile.

Chapter Twenty-two

SLOWLY I climbed the hill. The moon was up, the cars had found their parking-space, the streets were empty. There was no night-life in Assisi. Visibility was excellent, progress was easy, and I found the doorway of the chapel very soon, sooner than I wanted to, indeed, for I caught myself hesitating on the threshold, half-hoping that Perpetual Adoration stopped at midnight (did nuns ever go on strike?), and I should find the door shut.

But it wasn't. On entering I lurched a little, as the most sober person might have, confronted by the dark. I knelt down at once; the intention of the chapel required this, and besides, it helped me to get my bearings.

I said a prayer or two, and then looked up. There were the two poor Clares, or two others, to me indistinguishable from them, their heads bowed in adoration. And there, too, in the opposite pew to theirs, in the front row of devotion, so to speak, was the figure I had seen before, which must be Gilbert's.

But must it be? There was only one way of finding out, and much against my will I took it. I rose from my place, and stole along the row of pews until I reached the front one, opposite to his, and only a yard away from him. Then I knelt down. The nuns, away on my left, did not lift their heads.

I had decided that if he did not speak to me, then I would speak to him, in spite of the rule of the chapel, which, I supposed, enjoined the strictest silence, as their own rule enjoined silence on the Poor Clares. I saw the lips of the nun nearest to me move, but prayer was not the same as speech, for it was addressed to God, not man. I was grateful for their comfortable presence, as if it were a protection; Gilbert would be less likely to get up and make a scene with me if they were there.

I stole a look at him. His face was buried in his hands, and I could not see if his lips moved. There was nothing positive to recognize him by, as there had been, or had seemed to be before, when he turned his cheek towards me. I fancied I saw a faint gleam between his fingers, such as sometimes shows between the fingers of a man who strikes a match on a windy night to light his cigarette; but that is a rosy gleam, and this gleam, unless I imagined it, had the luminous pallor of a glow-worm.

I could not bring my mind to bear on adoration, and as the minutes fled I began to think of Myra: would she have woken up in terror, finding herself alone; and (a more practical and unworthy thought) would the porter have stayed up to let me in, since neither the townsfolk nor the visitors at Assisi kept late hours? I could not stay, I must not stay; yet how to leave the chapel until I had made sure that my neighbour on the right was, or was not, Gilbert? And, as often happens when one is forcing oneself to act against one's inclination, another part of myself developed an equally strong resistance to the project. The chapel itself seemed silently to protest against being used for a purpose for which it was not meant.

Supposing the figure was an hallucination, a projection created by my own state of mind, forced off its balance by the extreme emotions (among which guilt was present though hidden), of the past days and weeks? Myra hadn't seen it, though by nature she was more observant than I was.

The fingers moved; the phosphorescence between them brightened. I leaned across the aisle and whispered 'It is you Gilbert, isn't it?'

He made no answer, and summoning up my courage I said more loudly:

'Come outside, I want to talk to you.' It sounded like the challenge that one toper gives another in a public house.

At that he turned to me and gave me through his decaying marshlight mask a look so full of agony and reproach that I couldn't bear it and slid sideways into the aisle.

The nuns jumped up and exchanged a hurried, whispered word; then one of them came to me and helped me to my feet.

144

'E ammalato?' she asked, and then, guessing that I was English, 'are you eel?'

I laughed hysterically at the suggestion that I was an eel.

'Permit me to accompany you to the door,' she said, while her sister Clare (if Clare she was) returned to her devotions, almost as if nothing had happened.

I looked back towards Gilbert's pew, but it was empty. When we were on the pavement outside the chapel, I asked in halting Italian:

'Did you see anyone, a pale-faced man in black?'

'I saw no one,' she replied, 'but then we do not look about much—it is not the will of our foundress, Santa Chiara, nor the will of God. We try to keep our thoughts and eyes on one thing only. We saw you and heard you because we could not help it, but for us there is, or ought to be, only one Presence.'

'Does anyone come here who is unhappy?' I asked idly.

The nun shrugged her shoulders.

'Oh, signore, how can we tell? The soul has need of adoration, and perhaps most need when it is unhappy. I hope you are not unhappy?'

'Well, not very happy,' I said.

'Then perhaps it will have helped you, coming here,' she said, 'and I hope you will often come again.'

'In the flesh?' I asked her rashly.

'In the flesh or in the spirit. The spirit has more need of adoration than the flesh has.'

'Could I have come in without your seeing me?'

'Non credo, signore, but death is a mystery, and there may be spirits that we do not see. Ma sta bene? are you well?' she asked, anxiously. 'If not I will accompany you to your house, or to the hospital, se ne ha bisogno.'

I thanked her, and said I had no need of the hospital, and she went back into the chapel. I remained for a few moments on the threshold, looking up and down the street. It seemed to be quite empty, and I neither met nor was overtaken by anyone on my way to the hotel. The night-porter was still up and greeted me

with a smirk of complicity, as if I had returned from an assigna-
tion.

*

I had left Myra's door on the latch. I peeped in but she was still
asleep,—luckier than I, for though I gave myself the same
medicine that I had given her, and a stronger dose, I lay awake
till dawn.

Chapter Twenty-three

I PACKED my things before breakfast, to be ready to start off, but Myra surprised me by saying, 'Do you think we need go quite at once?'

She seemed to have recovered her composure, though there were black smudges under her eyes.

'As you wish,' I said, 'but we must go before twelve, you know, or they will charge us for an extra day. And besides,' I reminded her, 'Barbara may be coming, and you told me you didn't want to meet her.'

'Oh yes, Barbara, of course,' she answered, vaguely. 'I had forgotten about Barbara. But she couldn't get here before mid-day, could she? And I wanted to pay one more visit to San Francesco. And also to see the London papers.'

I didn't ask her why, but said, 'We can buy them at Spoleto.'

I knew then how preoccupied she was, but agreed that we should order the car for twelve o'clock, and punctually at twelve we started off, asking the driver to call at the newspaper shop in the Piazza on the way.

But there we drew a blank. The English newspapers had all been sold, the woman told us; 'there are so many English people here.'

On Myra's face the shadow deepened; from mine, I suppose, it lifted: anything for a respite, and no news was good news. And at Spoleto it was the same story: the *forestieri* had bought up all the English papers.

I could not get in touch with Myra: I had a miserable feeling that she was slipping from my grasp. We did a little desultory sight-seeing: we admired the Filippino Lippis in the Cathedral, but we could not concentrate on them, or on each other. The place was alive with tourists, fashionable, well-dressed people, motorists from Rome, on Festival bent, quite different from the humbler folk who thronged Assisi.

'Shall we try to get tickets for the Verdi Requiem?' I asked. 'They give it in front of the Cathedral. It should be wonderful.'

Myra assented, but all the tickets had been sold. We went up to our double room, and were trying to make plans for the evening, when suddenly the telephone bell rang.

'A call for you, signore.'

'I'll take it downstairs,' I said to Myra. 'I know you want to rest.'

Barbara's voice . . . 'You haven't heard the news?' she said.

'What news?'

'Oh, I thought you must have heard. You got my telegram, didn't you?'

'No,' I said. 'There was a telegram for me, but it . . . it miscarried. What was it about?'

'It was about Gilbert . . . He disappeared. I thought he might have gone out to Assisi, as he talked of doing, that's why I came. I thought—oh, I don't know what I thought. But it doesn't matter now. His body has been found—he's dead.'

'Oh Barbara, how terrible.'

'It's our fault really. Yours and mine and Myra's. He thought she had abandoned him, you see. He depended so much on her, and I . . . I couldn't fill her place. Need you have taken her from him, Edward?' I heard the tears in her voice.

'I didn't take her from him, as you call it, and I am inexpressibly shocked to hear of his death. But there was one thing that Gilbert never realized—'

'What was that?'

'That we all have our own lives to lead. Not only him.'

'Oh, don't say anything against him, please. He suffered so much. And he was so generous—generous to all of us. Not only in intention, but in fact. He gave me—'

'What?'

'Oh, just a nice teapot.'

'But did he give anything to Myra?'

'No. But I know what he *wanted* to give her, and it was because he couldn't—couldn't, because she was with you—that he gave up living.'

That was a gift indeed.

'What did he want to give her, Barbara?'

'I can't tell you now.'

At that moment we were cut off, and neither of us had the energy, or perhaps the wish, just then, to be re-connected.

*

We all three met the next morning, and began by saying as little as we could, but we agreed that we must go back at once to England.

'I'll see about getting us reservations for tomorrow,' I said. 'There must be an agency in Spoleto.'

'I got mine in Assisi,' Barbara said. 'They told me it was the last seat on the plane,' she added pointedly.

'What a pity,' I said, trying to sound sincere, 'that we can't all go together.'

Neither Myra nor Barbara made any comment on this. We looked at each other with hard, shut faces. I was the common enemy, I felt. From their different angles they turned their fire on me. They kept a little of it for each other, but I, I was the villain of the piece. This I resented; for what had Gilbert done for them, or they for Gilbert, except to encourage and prolong a situation which had nothing real in it, nothing of lasting emotional value, only a dependent selfishness on his side, (for he could not manage his own life alone) and on theirs a flattered vanity, which fed on which each thought she had done for him. They didn't like each other the better for that, either.

As our interview went on (it wasn't a conversation or a talk), it came out how much I had concealed from Myra. Barbara hinted, and Myra did not disagree, that I had lost her telegram on purpose: she had sent it as soon as she knew that Gilbert was missing, in the hope that Myra's immediate return would restore his mental balance. It was her last, desperate throw to get Myra back.

Barbara behaved with dignity, treating Myra and me as people she had long known but would not willingly see again. Myra rebelled against this and began to come round to my side; but then it came out, as it was bound to, and Barbara made sure that it should—the extent to which (as regards Gilbert) I had withheld the truth from Myra.

But for that—!

I had to hang my head in the presence of my two adversaries. Little as they liked each other, they liked me less. Barbara's words and tone implied that I had been a traitor all along; if I had not abducted Myra, Gilbert would still be thumping out on the piano the angry discords that characterized his music.

'He was at odds with himself,' said Barbara, 'but he relied on us,' (she gave a quick look to left and right) 'to see him through. The last day I saw him—I can't remember which day, but it doesn't matter, he told me something that surprised me. He told me that his Aunt Clare had made over the pictures, and the other things, to him years before she died, soon after her husband died, in fact. She showed the same foresight that he had,—she was not the wife of a businessman for nothing—so his Uncle Alfred's possessions twice escaped estate duty, and might have done so a third time, if Gilbert had lived long enough.'

Here Barbara stopped, to compose her features and control her voice which had grown husky. I think it was only our presence, and the animosity she felt towards us, that prevented her from breaking down.

'She left him the things outright, they were his to dispose of, and the people who said she had earmarked some of them for certain friends of his and hers were wrong.'

Here Barbara gave us a defiant glare, which again may have been a substitute for tears. They both looked straight ahead: Barbara had only benefited from Aunt Clare's will to the extent of a Crown Derby teapot. It was I who had to avert my eyes; but what after all was the value of the Girtin? Friends much less intimate with Gilbert than I was, who had done less and cared less for him than I had, in the days when he was unknown, had received much greater benefits.

Myra, defending me, reminded Barbara of this. 'And are you sure,' she said in a small steely voice, 'that Aunt Clare didn't want Gilbert to distribute some of her treasures? He told me that she had.'

The rivalry between the two women flared up in their eyes.

'I can only tell you what he said to me,' said Barbara. 'I may not have been as much in his confidence as you used to be.'

'Gilbert was never particularly truthful,' I put in, and was at once stung by my disloyalty. 'I got the same impression as Myra did, that his aunt didn't want him to keep everything himself.'

But my triumph was short-lived, when it gradually came out, as it was bound to do, that I had deceived Myra in all sorts of ways and withheld from her the written knowledge I had of Gilbert since she and I had eloped to Assisi. I couldn't deny that I had cut a poor figure, and that Myra thought so too: her face was changed towards me. Out of loyalty she tried not to let Barbara see it, but Barbara did.

'Perhaps you don't know, Edward,' she said, thrusting a finger towards me, 'why Gilbert wanted to dispossess himself of all these things? He might have been a rich man, almost a millionaire, if he had kept them.'

'I've no idea,' I said, as indifferently as I could. 'Gilbert's behaviour has always been a mystery to me, and his motives were no concern of mine,—or yours,' I added.

'How heartless you are, and how ungrateful,' retorted Barbara. 'You took his friendship for granted: you never bothered to find out what his real feelings were—nor did you, Myra. You just thought it was enough that Gilbert leaned on you.'

'What nonsense you talk,' said Myra, roused. 'I gave up my life—the better part of it—to Gilbert. You, Barbara, may have been watching from the wings, watching and criticizing, but you were never on the stage, or near it, although he used you as his secretary.'

'I know one thing about Gilbert,' said Barbara, 'which neither of you, perhaps—you are so taken up with each other—seems to know. He told me the last time I saw him—I don't remember when it was, and I don't want to.'

'A conveniently short memory,' I said.

'Perhaps, but not as short as some peoples'! He said that when he woke up in the morning he hated himself so much that he could hardly get up,—he felt utterly worthless, and there were hammers beating in his brain, as they do in his music, one against another. And he felt that if he could do some of his friends a good turn—'

'Oh, he was a do-gooder, was he?'

Barbara ignored me.

'He wouldn't feel that way when he woke up and was, as he said, such bad company for himself. And he thought his music would be the better for it, if he could create a harmony in himself—'

'Good Heavens,' I said.

'—by creating harmony around him. He always wanted harmony, or what passed for harmony in modern music, and by giving something to all his friends—'

'But, not to you,' I broke in, 'except for the teapot, and nothing at all to Myra.'

I let these exceptions linger in the air: Barbara, I felt was having things too much her own way, but she flashed back at me:

'No, he left his aunt's bequest to everyone who, he thought would like a *concrete* reminder of him.'

'Thank you,' I said, remembering that attack is the best form of defence, 'and I suppose he thought that you and Myra didn't need such material stimulants.'

Barbara said nothing and I suddenly noticed how desperately tired she looked after her long journey out from England yesterday,—London airport, Rome airport, the stifling heat in Rome railway station, the train rattling up through Italy to Foligno, the quick change at Foligno into the little electric train for Assisi that one had to jump on from the low platform, luggage in hand, —would Gilbert have been grateful to her for all this devotion?

Just another crash and bang, another expression of his impatience with himself and with the world.

We sat silent for a minute or two, trying to relate our private emotions to the larger problem that Gilbert represented. After all, he had been a great friend, a dear friend, to the three of us, and a benefactor to me, at any rate. Was it significant that, dying, he had brought about this clash between us, firm friends before, a discord that nothing could resolve?

Mild-mannered as he was, soft-hearted as he seemed to be, he had set us by the ears; we should never again see eye to eye as we once had. Could it be that his music was an instinctive expression of his deepest nature, which was always at odds with itself, and that his final bequest to us was to live out, in our now discordant lives, the symphony he had not been able to finish? Did the three of us, with our looks of ill-concealed hostility, represent a *trio antipatico* which Gilbert might have written? Brethren, what a joyful thing it is to dwell together in unity! We had lived in unity once, and look at us now!

'Was Gilbert religious, do you think?' I asked Barbara, trying to bring the conversation back to a more friendly tone. 'I never thought he was, but what you said about his waking up with these despairing thoughts—'

'I don't know,' she said, 'but now I think he may have been. The gifts, you know, and his Aunt Clare, whom he came to associate with her namesake at Assisi . . . He wanted some form of worship, I believe, that would have integrated him . . . and satisfied his spiritual aspirations, instead of being always at odds with himself. But if he ever found it, or if it brought him happiness, except in death—wasn't his wish to give also a token of reconciliation?'

'You may be right,' I said, 'you may be right. But he gave you nothing, Barbara?'

'Only the teapot.'

'And nothing to Myra?'

Barbara hesitated and looked at Myra. She didn't try to answer, so Barbara answered for her.

'He wanted to give her something, too, he told me so, but he couldn't, because—'

'Because of what?'

'Because you were here—you, Edward and Myra.'

'What did he want to give her?' I asked, though I knew the answer.

'His love, just his love. You see, he always adored her, and he proved it by dying. Dying was the form his adoration took.'

Myra burst into tears.

'I never knew,' she said between her sobs, 'I never knew. He never told me.'

Trying to comfort her, Barbara and I momentarily forgot our differences. But Myra was inconsolable: she wept and wept, until we looked away from her, embarrassed; but the waiters, who passed and repassed our table, gave her pitiful looks, and almost wept themselves.

'Gone,' I thought (as far as I could think of anything), 'gone with the wind is the conviction that I had at last forced Myra to accept, and useless, worse than useless, were the pains I had spent trying to persuade her that Gilbert was no good to her, he was only using her for his own selfish ends. By his death he had wiped out, for her, what was the truth, the real truth. The fact that I had been the gainer for the moment, by persuading her of this truth, didn't matter; anyone who wished her well, any disinterested person, even, would have done the same. The instinct for self-sacrifice, to which many women are a prey, when confronted by a forcible, but not all that talented male—had quite overcome her, just as her emotions had overcome her intellect, which was considerable.'

To my own part in the drama, my deceptions and evasions and deliberate misrepresentations, I did not give a thought.

'Shall we have another drink?' I asked at last. 'Barbara, you must be so tired, and Myra, you will feel better, perhaps, when you have brought some "physical aid to your moral consolation", as Burke put it.'

I felt that this intentionally unsympathetic appeal might bring Myra to her senses.

'No,' she sobbed. 'But you and Barbara—you have one.'

Barbara declined, so I ordered a drink for myself.

'I am sure Gilbert would have wished it,' I said, 'whatever else he was, he was a man, and wouldn't have thanked any of us for snivelling.'

Myra dried her tears. Barbara hadn't shed any, but they both looked at me with hatred, and together jumped up from the table, leaving me to pay the bill.

I confess that at the moment of paying it, or asking to pay it,—for a bill is not readily forthcoming in Italy—I wondered whom Gilbert had left his money to, the cash that his aunt had given him outright, besides the *objets* which he had or had not disposed of.

How would she have felt about all this, I asked myself, as I waited for the ladies to return, or (I looked at my watch, which said 3 o'clock) as I waited for them not to return. They professed to be angry with me; but were they not even angrier with each other and themselves? Was the conversation in the ladies' cloak-room or wherever they had retired to, going with a swing?

'Darling, he is the most awful man, I always knew it.'

'Yes, dearest, but you went on seeing him for all these years.'

'If I did, my pet, I was hardly more than a teen-ager when I met him, whereas you!'

Myra seemed to answer: 'Yes, angel, it has taken me less time than it took you to come to years of discretion.'

I waited for them on the beautiful terrace overlooking the beautiful street in the beautiful city of Spoleto.

'Bello—bello . . .' How much had we—Myra, Barbara and I—contributed to the *bellezza* of Italy? Precious little; but the country had no need of beauty, and quite enough wickedness to make our insignificant contribution show up like the traditional coal-streak on a negro's back.

The waiter brought the bill: he even brought the change. Half-pleased, half-disappointed by my tip (added to the service charge), he retired. How much more worth while would it have been to him, I thought, than the odd thousand lire, if Myra and Barbara had stayed behind, sprinkling the table-cloth with their tears! But, even in Italy, a public exhibition of emotion at a table in a restaurant, is not necessarily a money-spinner.

At last they appeared, eyelids darkened, lips brightened, faces powder-grey, conforming to the latest fashion.

I did not rise.

'Barbara would like me to go back with her,' said Myra, 'the concierge has been able to get a ticket for me. But it would make it easier if we both started from Assisi,—so I am going back there with her. The hotel seems to have a room for me,—or if not, we can share one. You, Edward, I suppose . . .'

'I shall make my own way back,' I said. 'And if either of you wants to see me, you know where to find me.'

Neither of them replied to this, as if it was too great an insult.

They were standing, each with bag in hand, in their travelling array. How they contrived to bring this transformation about, since Barbara's base was still at Assisi, I couldn't imagine.

'Bless you both,' I said, giving to the appearance of each the appreciation it deserved. 'And please be kind to each other. And remember, Myra, what you and I have meant to each other in the past few weeks.'

Barbara raised her shoulders, but Myra did remember, as the subsequent softening of her resentment towards me showed.

*

Poor Clare, poor Clare! I still had a day in hand, and I spent most of it at Assisi, in the church of Santa Chiara, with her unaltering and (I hoped) unalterable face turned towards me, meditating on her death and Gilbert's, and trying to reconcile myself to mine.